PRUDENCE BE DAMNED

'Hi, Dad. We have Ma, we want two hundred and fifty thousand dollars for her. This is, you know, for real, I mean we really do have her. Don't worry, right now she's perfectly safe, perfectly okay. I don't have to tell you what will happen if you call in the police. *I* wouldn't hurt her —naturally—but it's not just me that's involved . . .'

*Books you will enjoy
from Keyhole Crime:*

PRUDENCE
BE DAMNED

Mary McMullen

KEYHOLE CRIME
London · Sydney

*First published in Great Britain 1979 by
Robert Hale Limited*

Copyright © 1978 by Doubleday & Company, Inc.

Australian copyright 1981

*This edition published 1981 by
Keyhole Crime, 15-16 Brook's Mews,
London W1A 1DR*

ISBN 0 263 73710 1

*Made and printed in Great Britain by
Cox & Wyman Ltd., Reading.*

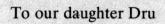

To our daughter Dru

The emptiness of his house, which he reached about midnight after the thirteen-and-a-half-hour nonstop flight from Tokyo a day earlier than he was expected, at first merely puzzled Hugh Devore.

He had tried to call from Kennedy but after his sixth occupied pay phone he impatiently abandoned the idea and went and found a cab.

He was very tired after the long journey and the round of ceremonies in Tokyo, where the new Sports Center by Devore Associates had been opened to much cutting of ribbons, bowing of dignitaries, commotion and heat and glare accompanying the television camera crews, pouring of scotch and sake and champagne.

Half listening to his third oration after a nine-course dinner topping a strenuous day, he had thought comfortingly of Madeline. Tit for tat, darling, he said to her mentally. Eminent Japanese architects made waves in the United States; he had just made a very large wave of his own in Japan's major city.

His house was on sharply angled Morton Street in Greenwich Village. Devore, when he bought and remodeled it, had kept the old handsome brick outer shell and stripped it naked inside. Even without human sounds and faces, it gave him a greeting feeling when he unlocked the front door. White heights, great spaces, a bridge flying airily overhead to link bedrooms, planked floors painted grass green throughout so that there was a country sunlit freshness at any hour of the day or night.

Greenness, whiteness. And silence.

One lamp was on in the living room, near the adventurous swoop of the staircase. He put down his bag, tossed his raincoat on a sofa, and went up the stairs.

Jane's room was the first on his right, door open, bed made and empty, clutter disposed of, as it was once a week on command from Madeline. Now at the age of twelve, to sleep at anyone's house but her own was one of her imperative pleasures. She was probably at the Bolands', two doors down on Morton Street. Madeline would know.

Rob's room was next. He had half hoped to find it looking permanently unoccupied. His week away would have been a suitable time for Rob to take himself off.

In April, on his nineteenth birthday, Rob had dropped out of Princeton with a resounding crash. He wanted, he said, to make films, and he was just wasting his time. There were several natural thunderstorms of quarrels. Then, in a way preconditioned but in spite of it still angry, Devore had said to him calmly and amiably, "You've heard the phrase 'cut off without a cent.' You can have a bed here and your meals—for the time being—and that's about it. If there's anything else you feel you need go out and earn some money."

"Doing what?"

"Oh, I don't know. Go play a piano at a resort in the Catskills, you're good at that. Or join a road gang and get a tan. Whatever you please. You will no doubt enjoy being completely on your own. Let's say by early June, no later."

Today was the tenth of June.

He was obviously, while not at home, still in residence. Tie dangling over the footboard of the brass-railed bed, familiar sweet smoky odor, empty beer can on the bedside table, lazy dent of a head on the pillow under the tweed spread.

Not for golden, blue-eyed, handsome Rob the scruffy blue jeans and dirty bare feet and blowing tangled hair, nor the anywhere bed or sleeping bag, and reliance on his peers for a handout of soup, wine, a joint.

He liked pleasant surroundings, good food, good if exotic clothing; when Devore had seen him last he had been attired in an immaculately tailored hacking-jacket suit of pale blue velveteen.

Inevitably, Devore had had his moments of wondering if his son was a homosexual, incipient or practicing. But he concluded sourly that it was perhaps more of a case of being born out of his time, a misplaced eighteenth-century young rake who would have loved to go about caped and sworded, wining and whoring and dueling.

He was not without precedent in the Devore lineage. Devore's paternal grandfather was never, although three times married, without a mistress, or several, openly maintained. He had once shot his valet in the foot when a favorite silk shirt was scorched by the pressing iron. He had had a long wicked merry life, his fortune not run through until the very edge of his grave, which he entered at the age of ninety.

Okay, Rob, he said to himself, tomorrow morning then. Hail and farewell, for a while. For a summer.

He crossed the flying bridge, turned right, and went to their room, the big back bedroom overlooking the long garden. Empty, although he knew that before he pushed wide the half-open door. He could always sense his wife's presence, rooms away from him.

The bed had an odd look; not peaceful. Blue and white striped sheets tossed like a troubled sea, a head's imprint on one striped pillow, a book fallen, open, on the floor.

Thrusting aside swift instinctive alarm, he picked up the book and put it on the white drum table beside the bed, neatly, as though to erase the idea of any kind of strangeness, violence, here upon the bed.

He even noted the title and author. *Left Hand, Right Hand!*

by Sir Osbert Sitwell. She had read it years ago, he remembered; she must have returned to it in some kind of leisurely page-ruffling peace.

There was probably a perfectly simple explanation for the bed.

The confusion of sheets, so unlike Madeline, might merely mean a restless afternoon nap.

Or . . . he'd read, in Japan, that an early heat wave had struck the east coast; perhaps she had cut and run for their weekend house in Greens Farms, Connecticut.

She'd leave a note somewhere, of course, Madeline of the delicate lovely manners. Perhaps on the slate in the kitchen, and he felt himself wanting a drink anyway. The kitchen would be the place to look.

There wasn't any scribble on the slate. He poured scotch, got out ice cubes, and stood looking around the big shining efficient room. No untidiness here, either dinner had not been eaten or had been thoroughly cleaned up afterward.

He opened the dishwasher. Three of everything. The peacock-patterned dinner plates, salad plates, three settings of rosewood-handled stainless steel, three of the demitasse cups and saucers marbled in gold on white porcelain. As a rule, dinner dishes from the night before were put away in the morning, while she was making coffee.

The silence of his solid and beautifully insulated house pressed hard on his ears.

He looked in every conceivable place a note might be and found none, and then he went obsessively back to the bedroom.

It smelled of her, floating, gardeny.

She was not given to erratic behavior, any sudden seizing of the impulse of the hour. He wondered for one wild moment if there had been an act of love, here on this worrying bed, and if she had gone off with the man.

What man?

And if she, impossibly, had, wouldn't there be a "Dear Hugh" note for him?

He tried to remember how she had been, how she had looked, felt, before he left for Tokyo, his third trip since his design had triumphantly won him the Sports Center.

Used as she was to kissing him goodbye for Dallas, for Barbados, for Vancouver, she had been attempting as far as he could see to cope with her suddenly young and warm forlornness at the separation.

Her head coming just to his shoulder, and pressed briefly into it, her arms very tight around him. Long sleeveless black dress which emphasized her astonishing fairness, a luminous and healthy, lightly freckled pallor. Pale, almond-shaped eyes under the rounded innocent high forehead, pale red-fair hair with a faint shiny crimp to its texture, caught back in a high small chignon, short fine nose.

Long ago, he had heard Rob complain to Jane, "Why does Ma have to look like a picture in a museum or something? Why doesn't she look like everybody else?"

"Since when is everybody else what everyone wants?" Jane asked, in confused defense.

Entering and exiting from the conversation, Devore had said to Rob, "I'm sorry I failed to provide you with your idea of a mother who's just folks."

The soft helpless crumple of a thin blue robe over a chair arm, the bowl of fresh white marguerites on the dressing table, the blue slippers shed at the bedside, caused him as well as worry a pang of guilt at his wild and fleeting suspicion.

As far as he knew, and he thought he knew her well after twenty years, they had an unusually sound and happy marriage.

The closet door was slightly open. He went over and without thinking why touched the black linen dress she had worn to say goodbye in, and a silvery-green shimmer of flounced silk, a dress he loved on her.

This was ridiculous. Reduce it to the molehill it was.

Ruthlessly disregarding the hour, he began telephoning their friends. She almost never, at night, went out without him. She admitted to being mildly antisocial and was more than content in bed with her book until her usual drifting-off time, one o'clock or so.

He called the Connells, the Bolands, the Guedellas, the Norgords, the Brodericks (not at home), and got variously vague, highballed, sleepy, or startled "nos" from those he talked to. Anything wrong, Hugh? No, nothing wrong—just trying to track down my wandering wife, she didn't expect me until tomorrow.

He was informed that Jane, as he had thought, was safely asleep at the Bolands'.

After a little hesitation, he went ahead and roused his neighbor, Trent, in Greens Farms. Next door, but several acres away. Sorry to trouble him, but did he know if Madeline had arrived sometime late in the day, or in the evening?

"Absolutely not." Trent yawned. He was a gossip and scented a large dramatic quarrel. "I had occasion to visit your place, outside it, that is, I have to confess I stole an armload of your roses, the yellow ones, blushing unseen, as it were. And I helped myself to some gypsophila to go with them, you'll be glad to know the garden's looking well. The house was pitch dark, no car, nothing."

He hadn't thought until now to check the garage because she disliked driving and preferred even the cranky train to the hour and a half on the Cross County and Merritt parkways.

He found himself running down the stairs and deliberately slowed his feet. You could create a very real panic for yourself if you worked at it.

There was probably, he repeated, a perfectly simple explanation.

He went out through the kitchen into the dark garden. A grape arbor made a thickly canopied green tunnel from the back door to the garage, which was on the ground floor of a house he had bought on the street above, Barrow, and which was now in the process of being remodeled to be rented as apartments. There was room for three cars in the garage. His Mercedes was there, silently shining, and the red Ford convertible given to Rob on his eighteenth birthday by a doting great-aunt.

Rob. Cars— Someone else's car? The sound just then of a faraway siren struck him over the heart. An accident, a telephone call or the police at the door, Madeline rushing out of the house, of course no time for a note, waiting now in some ghastly waxed hospital corridor, or holding the hand of a dying boy—

Stop it.

But if something frightful had happened to Rob, she wouldn't call her husband at home because she didn't know he was there.

He moved a hand over his face as if to rearrange and calm his features and went back to the kitchen and poured another drink.

On hazard, not wanting to see what he was looking for, he slid back a mirrored door in the hall and examined the top shelf of the deep broad closet. Her small suitcase, the dark blue canvas one bound in ivory leather, was missing.

"Dear Hugh, I don't know how to break this to you but . . ."

Except it hadn't been written.

Maybe it would be a telephone call, tomorrow, when he was expected back.

"Darling—I'm so sorry—I thought it would be better to talk to you, say it, instead of just writing it down—"

But you couldn't do it, not you, Devore said, and wondered for a bad moment if he had spoken aloud.

Among other things, leaving out love, constancy, a transparency about her, an essential innocence, she was in her own relaxed way a Roman Catholic, given to the observance of thou-shalt-not's.

Himself an agnostic, he heard the words forming in his head, Oh God, don't let—

Don't let what? What dreadful surprise, what disaster, was waiting, until time unfolded it and presented it to him?

Possibly Jane had borrowed the suitcase and forgotten to put it back.

To defy the dangerous echoing silence, he turned on the radio. Saint-Saëns's *Danse Macabre*. He spun the dial. A telephone talk show, a woman's voice, "I have this terrible lumbago and I wonder if any of your listeners could—" A pop station, "Up, up, and away-y-y . . . come fly with me in my beautiful balloon . . ."

He stood in the exact center of his living room, hands in his pockets, studying the design of the Bokhara underfoot. He was tall, with untidy thick dark hair, a strong face lit when not under stress by witty gray eyes behind glasses heavily rimmed in tortoise. His nose and jaw were well cut and forthright, and his air that of a man courteously but firmly expecting to have things pretty well his own way. He looked faintly travel-rumpled, his body big and powerful under the pencil-striped dark suit.

He was not at all good at any time at being patient, and waiting for things, or standing in line for anything.

Go ahead, thrust aside the fantasies, do what's sensible, normal, and everything will sooner or later shake itself out, into its proper place and shape.

Remind himself, *remind* himself, that on her calendar he wasn't to be home for another twenty-four hours. Why shouldn't she be out, free, amusing herself?

But. But. The largest but, the look of interrupted repose about the bed. Madeline in the normal course of things didn't leave unmade beds behind her.

A hasty rising, a sudden packing of a suitcase—why?

"Why" and "but" teamed up uncomfortably.

He went upstairs, undressed, put on a robe, doused his face in cold water, dried it, and stared at the man in the medicine-cabinet mirror who had assumed for comfort a false, everything's-all-right smile.

Back down to the kitchen. The peculiar feeling in his ribs might have something to do with hunger.

A slice of Vermont cheddar, and an English water cracker. Indigestion struck knifelike the moment he'd gotten it down.

Bicarbonate of soda. One-third of a teaspoon to half a glass of water. His drink to freshen. That might help, too.

A good idea, fighting exhaustion, to stretch out on the sofa in the living room. Near the hall, the front door, just in case—

It was a very comfortable sofa, from Sweden. Sheets and blanket weren't needed in the controlled temperature and humidity of the house. Any true rest, deep and forgetful, was out of the question. But he'd be there, and the puzzle pleasantly over, if and when the key turned in the lock, Madeline's key.

"Darling, you do live dangerously. You know you can't eat cheese late at night."

He was, finally, in an uneven nightmared sleep when the call came, at 4:30 A.M.

Rob.

Deep crisp inherited Devore voice a little higher than normal, sounding surprised, breathless.

"Hi, Dad." Brief pause, breath almost regained. "We have Ma, we want two hundred and fifty thousand dollars for her— What did you say?"

Devore had made some kind of noise but hadn't formed a word.

"This is, you know, for real, I mean we really do have her. Don't worry, right now she's perfectly safe, perfectly okay. I don't have to tell you what will happen if you call in the police. *I* wouldn't hurt her—naturally—but it's not just me that's involved. And at this place, we have a clear view of the approach roads like, you know, looking down from a helicopter."

Devore heard himself ask, in the manner of the village idiot, "Where are you calling from?"

"Nowhere. Ma is safely . . . nowhere. Are you still there?"
He had no idea how long his silence had lasted.

"You're absolutely mad," he said.

"No, sane as chickens with their heads on. I'll be in touch tomorrow—no, it's today, isn't it? right!—about the details. And don't bother to have the FBI or whatever cutting into the phone line, listening, because it won't be done by phone."

And then, in a voice run out of breath again and overtaken by a tremor, "Well, I guess that's about it. Night, Dad."

2

Madeline Devore was astonished when Rob called her, at five, and said, "Mind if I bring a girl around to dinner, Ma?"

It hadn't happened for years and she wasn't entirely pleased that it was going to happen now. It wasn't his, or his generation's, way. They would no doubt bore one another half senseless. The girl would look at her as if she were something preserved under glass.

"Of course not, when shall I expect you?"

"Around six . . ." And in partial explanation, just when after all she was beginning to feel a little flattered, "She saw the pictures of the house in *The New York Times Magazine* and wants to take a look."

Don't be caught arranging petunias from the garden or baking the corn bread Hugh often ate slit and crisply toasted for breakfast; like someone out of *Woman's Day*. Both of which she had wanted to do before she mixed herself an icy dry martini.

She was freshly bathed, dressed in white linen pants and tunic; she supposed he would find her presentable. It might be a good idea to put something on her bare feet. A pair of white thong sandals.

Waiting for them, she heard her husband's voice in her ears, something he had murmured to her when he was half asleep, sounding troubled, musing, "I love him, you know, but right now I don't particularly like him . . ."

The front door opened, letting in a gush of damp heat and a heavy smell of car exhaust.

Rob, in an immaculate black mechanic's coverall, long straight golden hair falling silkily from a center parting, eyes radiantly blue, his father's commanding nose but a more delicate version of it. His skin was very fair but in summer effortlessly acquired a rich apricot tan against which his white teeth sparkled splendidly.

"Evening, Ma, this is Margaret Aston, better known to all and sundry as Mouse."

The girl was almost as tall as six-foot Rob, lean rather than slender, in close-cut jeans and a loose pink shirt. Her skin was scrubbed, fresh, and without makeup, her glistening brown hair worn like Rob's but longer. The tight lifting curve of her lips suggested faint, secret amusement. Her eyes were very dark and curiously lightless, steady and heavy in their gaze upon Rob's mother.

I am being very thoroughly, and at her leisure, weighed, measured, assessed, Madeline thought, and wondered a little about it.

"Nice to meet you, Mrs. Devore."

Sometimes Madeline's special antennae—tendrils feeling the air about her, finding out what other people were really thinking, feeling, wanting—was a help to her and sometimes she wished it would switch off.

She got from the lean quiet girl a scent of danger.

Annoyed at herself, brushing it away, she said, "There are all kinds of cold things to drink . . ."

"She doesn't, but I'll get a beer and some kind of her own slop—"

"I'd like a glass of milk, Robbie," Mouse said, her eyes fixed on Madeline's martini glass.

Good, then; no long interval trying to find things to talk about, over sips. Fifteen polite minutes while the girl, on and off, remembered her milk and Rob downed Swedish beer. The two made no attempt whatever at conversation. Madeline did as well as she could: the weather, and where was Mouse from? Oh, Greenwich, Round Hill, yes, they had friends there, in fact had spent a weekend in May with them—

"I mean, that's where I used to live way back when," Mouse said, her calm voice dismissing background, home, parents.

Madeline finished her drink and got to her feet. "You said Mouse wanted to see the house." She hoped her mild disbelief didn't show in her voice; it was inconceivable to her that Rob's girl had any aesthetic interest in the premises. "Suppose you show her around—and the garden—while I get dinner."

Jane called while she was whipping a pinch of curry into the lemon mayonnaise for her shrimp salad. "I'm at Elizabeth's, she wants me to stay over, may I?"

"Yes, don't stay up too late—Rob's here with someone named Mouse."

Jane, always direct, said, "I don't like her, do you?"

"I've just met her. I'll see you in the morning."

Odd. The circles occupied by Jane and Rob were worlds apart. How and where had Jane met her? It gave her a peculiar small feeling of discomfort to think he might have had her here, in this house she professed she wanted to see, at some previous time when his mother was out of it.

Dinner was burdensome.

Mouse ate silently and tidily, without comment or compliment. The shrimp salad, tomatoes in oil and basiled vinegar, a basket of thin airy toast with Parmesan butter, cold cantaloupe halves filled with raspberries in sour cream. Fork steadily inserting food into the curved contained mouth as though she were fueling, not dining. If Hugh had been there, chilled white wine would have appeared. This, however, did not proclaim itself—why?—as a festive occasion, but instead something they all felt had to be gotten through.

Rob surprised her by saying, "You sit down, Ma, we'll clear the table and get the coffee. Large? Or demitasse as usual?"

"Thank you, demitasse."

I wonder, she thought, if at my advanced age I can make it to the living room unassisted. But it was, yes, unexpectedly nice of him.

Even though the coffee when served to her in the marbled white and gold cup wasn't good. Espresso, not fragrant and aromatic as it should be but overstrong, rank, bitter. What on earth could you do to freshly ground coffee from the Italian market on Bleecker Street to make it taste like this?

She finished it as quickly as possible, hoping that at the last hot gulp she hadn't grimaced. Rob's eyes on her looked anxious.

"Delicious," said his polite mother.

"Well . . ." Rob drained his own coffee. "We're off. Thanks for the food, Ma."

"Thank you very much, Mrs. Devore," Mouse said. She was standing several feet away and Madeline got again the whiff of danger. And along with it now a cold undisguised dislike, coming at her.

She asked herself briefly if the dislike was personal, or merely a blanket hostility toward the next generation up, perhaps with specific reference to people's mothers. It didn't matter. Mouse was probably very far from the last in Rob's long parade of girls.

It was pleasant to be rid of the dark presence.

She turned on music, put the dishes in the dishwasher, tidied and washed the blue and white tiled counters, flicked crumbs off the cutting board, put a leftover half cantaloupe into the refrigerator in a wrap of waxed paper, and wondered at the weight of her hands, suddenly so heavy on her wrists.

At a little after nine she went yawning up the whirl of stairs. Disgraceful at this hour to feel so sleepy, so completely shot. Maybe it had something to do with their putting her in the ranks of the elderly, someone whose President might have been Warren Harding.

"You sit down, Ma, we'll clear the table . . ."

It was more likely that she was just badly missing Hugh. His being anywhere in the house sent a vibrancy through it, an electric current. Very nice to stay awake to.

Wanting and needing some kind of contact with him, she went for a moment into his studio, to the left of their bedroom, put a hand to the surface of the big drawing board, emptied a forgotten ashtray, picked up a pencil and wrote on his pad, "Compliments of a friend." And then, yawning again, went into the bedroom, undressed, tried to remember if she had brushed her teeth yet and couldn't, gave them a possible second brushing, and got into bed.

She managed two pages of Osbert Sitwell before she fell deeply and heavily asleep.

What happened afterward revealed itself only in oddly brilliant patches. As though you were walking in dark woods with a defective flashlight that kept going on and off. Or watching a badly projected movie, the sound failing along with the picture.

Hands upon her. Not Hugh's. In her pit of sleep, she had been safely in his arms.

Invading hands, not cruel but not welcome and warm and kind.

Coming down a long tunnel, a voice from a great distance away, "No—don't switch the light off, we have to *see*—and besides there's no real point in it unless she knows it's you."

A familiar voice, someone she'd met somewhere.

Her head being lifted from the pillow, something impossibly being thrust, balled up, into her mouth. A handkerchief. The scent or taste of starch on her palate, along with the intruding dry strangling cloth.

She was strong, slender, and in very good physical shape; as she began to writhe and kick, her legs were sat upon and she felt a pressure of hard buttocks on her knees.

Her enraged arms were held flat on the bed by Rob, bending over her, his golden hair swinging straight down.

His eyes were anxious again, as when he had watched her drinking her coffee.

"Relax, Ma, nobody wants to hurt you . . ."

A plunge of the presence seated upon her knees, a shining brown swoop—hair—a careful searching of the inside tender place in an arm held tight by Rob, a thin delicate prick. A mosquito, a bee—wasn't it time to wake up?

And say to Hugh, "Oh, thank God, darling—it isn't real—I had this ghastly dream . . ."

She was lifted from the bed and sensed rather than saw herself wrapped in the pink summer blanket like a new baby.

"Got everything?" Known, and stranger's, voice above her head, strong arms cupping her under shoulders and knees. He didn't sound like himself. The creamy confidence was missing.

"Yes . . . the light?"

"Leave it on. She reads until one usually."

The flashlight flickered, the screen dimmed. Grape leaves seemed to be touching her hair as she was hastily carried through another echoing tunnel.

Mouse laughed at the last three words from the bundle placed on the floor of the back seat of the car she had borrowed for them.

"Look here, Rob," Madeline Devore said in her soft direct beautiful voice, to her son.

After that, for a considerable time, she said nothing.

3

"I hope you know what you were doing, with that needle."

Keeping the car at an exact fifty-five miles an hour on the Garden State Parkway, he spoke over his shoulder to Mouse, in the back seat. She sat curled into a corner, a .32 Colt revolver held lightly but awarely in her hand.

"It's too late to worry now," she answered him casually. "In for a penny, in for a pound, my dear old daddy used to say. But okay, yes, I did know what I was doing. More or less. She'll be good for five or six hours."

The kidnapping had been Mouse's idea. Or so she claimed.

Immediately after dropping out of college, he had begun thinking about the film he was going to make. He had wanted to call it *Me and Mouse* but she corrected the title to *Mouse and Me*.

He had met her at a party a week before he left Princeton. She was with a dangerous-looking man in his twenties called Al Madonna. He was immediately attracted to the calm recklessness she projected, the lean racy body, the compelling eyes.

Al Madonna had to leave New Jersey for Detroit the following day and Rob took over.

"That Madonna—you're not really his girl?"

"No," Mouse said. "Jersey junk, is what he is. Just a friend. Fun, though."

Mouse and Me was to be extemporaneous, made up and shot as they went along, a record of their days and nights, their wanderings. Several scenes in bed had already been recorded on film by an obliging friend. There were sequences in Chinatown and Hoboken, and one in Nantucket, where they had traveled on her funds.

Mouse said it was great, she'd never been in a movie before.

When his father informed him of the cutting off of any and all money, and stated rather than proposed his leaving the house and getting a job, she was furious. The film to be left hanging, Rob to be snatched from her side. She thought about it for a while.

"Hey, Rob, I have an idea."

Pretty funny idea to come from someone named Mouse.

She had told him how she came by her nickname. "I was, like, the quietest best little girl who was ever born." She was an only child of wealthy parents in Greenwich, Connecticut. "Nose in a book, straight A's, honor roll, valedictorian at my graduation. Glasses, not contact lenses like now. I needed them when I was ten and when I put them on Daddy said I looked like a dear little Beatrix Potter mouse in spectacles, and called me that from then on. I never bothered to change it back to Margaret, in a way it's fun."

"And when did you start to turn rotten?" Rob had asked amiably, interested in her history.

"Sometime in the summer after graduation. I'd passed my college entrance exams and mother took me—*took* me—shopping to Lord and Taylor to get clothes and things. And all of a sudden I thought, screw college, screw you, screw everything, and while *she* was trying on a pair of shorts, imagine, at her age, I ran off and took a bus down to the Village where a boy I knew in Stamford had moved to, his parents were in Europe and he was all alone in this great big apartment on West Eleventh Street. End of autobiography. *They* send me a check every month and keep wanting me to come home, or at least write. Sometimes I send them a postcard. I don't want the money to dry up."

But it wasn't enough money to keep both her and Rob. She shared an apartment on Leroy Street with two other girls; the check just about covered her rent, clothing, food and drink and entertainment.

" . . . Hey, Rob, I have an idea. I mean, I dare you . . ."

The suggestion had come toward the end of a long forty-eight-hour party. It had its good moments and its bad, which in their darkness were illuminated with flash and flare. They drifted, ten or so of them, from apartment to apartment. At one point they were in someone's loft, bare bodies strewn about the floor, clothes tossed any which way in corners or over easels. The music was too loud even for Rob's ears, a fist pounding your head. Later there was a good deal of confusion about whose jeans were whose. Mouse was not, at the time, Rob's partner. She kept appearing and disappearing, in and out of the party. And then she was back—after how many hours?—pink and gleaming, taut and cross-legged, leaning against his hip.

" . . . I mean, I dare you . . ."

Her voice sounded unreal, an echo under it. Or was it the words she was murmuring that were unreal? A dream maybe?

For a few seconds he was appalled at what she was—if she was real, alive, and beside him—proposing.

Then there was an excitement under his ribs and his head seemed to clear brilliantly, showing him what to do about his father and all that bust-up, finishing things, earn-your-way crap. His father was loaded; and earned more every hour on the hour.

He got to his feet with an effortless dancer's leap and felt as though he were continuing up into the air, over the living room, which now turned out to be almost empty, two boys tangled in sleep on somebody's white sofa, a blond girl prone, dazedly reading what looked to be the Bible, big red initial letters, ribbons dangling from it, in front of a wall of books.

He stretched long and triumphantly and reached down a hand to Mouse. In a strong if belated dealing with her assumption of initiative, power, and authority, he said coolly, "Funny the way you and I always think of the same thing at the same time. Actually, I happened to have that idea yesterday." Wrong, yesterday had been lost somewhere, or mislaid. "Or the day before. I was just kind of working it out. I was going to ask you to help, I don't think it could be a one-man job."

"I'll help," Mouse said.

After that, of course, there was no way out.

No, say that again, he told himself, fix that. I mean, from now on in there is no way but right straight ahead.

The house was in northwestern New Jersey, a few miles away from a little town called Prudence.

It had belonged to Mouse's Aunt Grace and she had visited there in summers as a child. Grace Aston had died during the past winter and her brother and heir, living in Italy, put it on the market.

So far there were no takers. It was huge, Victorian, dark, forbiddingly cupolaed and porched. Too big to be run without servants or by a family endowed with many eager helpful out-of-date children, and too small to be taken over as a seminary or nursing home.

It stood in six acres of steeply rising meadows and woodland, at the end of a winding drive bordered with rhododendrons, at a long remove from the narrow, little-traveled Bellamy Road. Developers cast greedy eyes on the land but Prudence was a town of the very rich and was severely zoned.

In addition to these drawbacks, the house was believed by local residents to be haunted. Children dared each other to creep up to the porches and peer through the screens.

The neglected great lawns were deep in daisies and buttercups. Immense weeping Norway spruces crowded darkly towering over the roofs.

There was a barn where horses had once been kept, and a separate four-car garage with chauffeur's quarters over it.

There was a springhouse, which they'd considered on one of their several preliminary explorations of the premises. No, too cold, Rob said, I mean really.

There was a little bedroom high in a cupola, reached by a narrow staircase, isolated—

"Ma's no athlete, but she's pretty good on her feet. She might break a window and somehow or other climb down."

In the cavernous underground warren—furnace room, laundry room, storeroom, cook's quarters—there was a wine cellar.

Perfect, they said in unison.

One door, heavy, tight-fitting, with a massive bolt and a padlock which had been left hanging open. No windows. The air in it fresh enough, not too cool, not too warm.

All set, then.

"What if someone wants to look at the house, after all it's for sale?" Rob asked.

"Well, with the cellar, and the ghost"—Mouse giggled—"makes it more fun, you know? And I have a perfect right to be here, with a friend, it's my own aunt's house, same name and everything."

He kept looking into the driving mirror, the muscles of his stomach, not just his ears, tensed and waiting for the raucous pursuing sirens, motorcycles, or a red-flashing knowing accusing car.

"You. Pull over to the side of the road."

In one of his many examinations of the mirror, he saw Mouse's hand with the black gun in it, raised to her hugely yawning mouth.

"Is that thing loaded?"

"Of course. What would be the point otherwise?"

This bothered him. His mother was in no circumstances to

be endangered, hurt. Skipping over the first necessary violence, the scene in the bedroom that he was already erasing from his mind—the eyes, God, her eyes—this whole thing was, well, just, a caper, sort of.

No sirens. No flashing red roof lights. Lumbering buses, trailer trucks, going about their nighttime business; nothing much in the way of traffic otherwise.

He turned off the Garden State and drove west. Returning to the gun as to a sore tooth, he said, "Well, but you've probably never shot off a gun, have you?"

"No, but it can't be all that difficult, you just point and pull this trigger . . . I wish I had some nice cold milk, I suppose we shouldn't stop somewhere for a second . . . ?"

"No stopping."

It made him a little nervous that it was all so simple, that everything was going so smoothly. Not a sound from the floor in back of him.

"Feel her pulse, is it okay?"

Pause. "It's all right, I think, and I put my hand in front of her mouth and she's breathing."

The town of Prudence looked soundly asleep as they drove through it. The rich within and around it did not allow roadhouses, dispensers of hamburgers and chocolate milk shakes, or slums.

An oval village green, white columns of a church caught in the headlights. A prim brick building, Prudence Township Library, with a cat stalking down its brick walk.

It was close to midnight. They had taken her out of the house at a little before ten-thirty, through the kitchen and under the grape arbor to the garage, where the gray Chevrolet borrowed by Mouse was parked.

He switched on the radio; rock shrieked in the quiet night and he turned the volume down.

"Turn it back up," Mouse demanded.

"Are you crazy?"

"And now, the news . . ." Disasters were muttered at them,

fire and death, an earthquake, the assassination of an American diplomat in an African country he'd never heard of, the crash of a cable car in the Alps, fourteen people believed dead, rescue parties . . .

"Seems like everybody has it rough," Mouse remarked, lazily.

"Shut *up*," straining his ears, waiting for the words: The wife of the well-known architect Hugh Devore is missing from her home at . . . But they weren't spoken, and how could anyone know this early in the game anyway? Jane was at her friend's house, his father half a world away. The cleaning woman didn't come until, let's see, the day after tomorrow.

"And now, the weather . . ."

He switched off the radio, feeling a slight easing in the ache of his stomach muscles.

Bellamy Road, now. Almost there. A car close behind them, headlights dazzling in the driving mirror. He pulled over and slowed to let the car pass. No passengers, just the driver, a man, staring straight ahead of him, not turning to peer into the gray car to see what might be on the floor in back.

He crawled until the car's lights disappeared, picked up speed for a mile, slowed again and turned into the driveway to the house.

On their first trip out, they had broken one of the bottom panes in the kitchen-door window to get at the Yale lock. He drove to the back of the house and stopped the car at the door. He'd rehearsed it all in his mind, only then there hadn't been a real body, heavy with sleep, in his arms.

She weighed about one hundred and twenty-five pounds.

"As soon as you get the door open, take her feet, Mouse," he whispered. There were no near neighbors to see lights and the house was invisible from the road. Mouse flicked a switch and the huge kitchen, clean except for ceiling corner cobwebs, sprang reassuringly out of the black tree-sighing night.

The cellar stairs led down from the kitchen. They maneuvered their burden down the stairs, across the laundry room, through a long cool shelved passageway, to the wine cellar, pulling light cords as they went.

The solid, planked door opened under Mouse's hand without a creak. Everything was in readiness for the cellar's new tenant; none of their arrangements had been disturbed.

An inflated plastic air mattress in the corner farthest from the door, against the stone wall. On it, a clean white sheet, a pillow, and a folded blue blanket. Beside it, a step stool used for reaching wine on high racks, pressed into service now as a table.

The step stool held a thermos bottle of cold water, a box of paper tissues, three Georges Simenon paperbacks he hoped his mother had not yet read, an immense volume of the plays of Shakespeare from the library upstairs ("What do you think this is," Mouse had said, mocking his preparations, "the Prudence Hilton? You've forgotten the Gideon Bible"), a box of saltines if hunger struck between meals, a jar of instant coffee in case she should wake early, before breakfast was brought to her, a small round clock also brought from the library, and a striped zipped waterproof case containing a new toothbrush, toothpaste, deodorant, a bottle of aspirin tablets, and a lipstick.

Nearby was a card table discovered in the laundry room, and a shabby comfortable basket chair from the cook's quarters.

They placed her, still blanket-wrapped, on the plastic mattress and bent over her, studying the closed eyes, the eyelashes, no, not so much as a quiver. He thought she was terribly white but then she was always pale in a healthy light-shining way.

Her breathing was soft and even.

What if, during the long night, it turned out that Mouse after all didn't know what she had been doing, with her needle?

He suddenly couldn't bear to keep looking at her, down there helpless on the mattress on the bare stone floor.

If you turned your eyes away from a thing, it would stop worrying you, take care of itself, no point in driving yourself crazy, she'd just sleep, and sleep, and in time wake up.

She would probably start screaming when she did wake up. It would be a natural thing to do. He knew he would be able to hear her, from the kitchen; he had had Mouse practice a single scream from behind the closed door of the wine cellar. It sounded muffled, far away, but he heard it.

"Come on, let's go," he said. "You bring down a thermos of hot water for the coffee so it'll be there when she wants it. And I see there's no spoon, bring that too. I'll go out to the car and get her suitcase and then I need at least two beers in a hurry."

He looked up at the naked light bulb in the ceiling and said, "Whoever's in here last, leave that on. I mean, to wake up in the dark—"

They had stocked one of the two refrigerators with food and drink. He opened his beer and drank deeply and thirstily from the can while Mouse heated water on the big white electric stove. Lucky it wasn't gas, it would have been turned off long ago.

Mouse went downstairs with the thermos of hot water, came back up again, made herself a thick ham sandwich and poured a glass of milk.

For a moment there seemed to be nothing to say to each other.

Feeling winded, exhausted, and not wanting to think of anything in particular, he opened another beer.

They had arranged that they would take turns, sleeping and waking, in the bedroom they would more or less share, the first one at the right at the top of the stairs. He thought there was no point in being this tired this early, Mouse would get to go to bed first.

She finished her sandwich and milk and came over to him.

"Kiss me good night, you cool cool criminal, you. Hey, we made it—congratulations to both of us."

"Don't say that. You'll jinx us." He began kissing her in a blurred desperate search for warmth and contact and she said, "That's enough, we can't do anything about it, at least not now. I'm off. *Don't* go to sleep, Robbie."

"I won't."

After she left him he went, very much against his will, down to look at his mother again. Breathing still, softly, regularly. As he watched, she changed the position of her body, very slowly. She had been lying on her back and now she turned on her side. One arm reached out in a groping motion and then relaxed over the edge of the mattress. The lashes didn't move.

He allowed himself a third beer. There was a big comfortable rocker, with a footstool, beside a well-curtained window. He sat down in it and put his feet up.

To keep awake, he read a cookbook from a shelf of such volumes by the kitchen door. In the middle of "Coquilles St. Jacques," he fell asleep. He had terrible dreams in which his father figured largely.

And then one, somehow the worst of all. He was on a train that had forgotten how to stop, relentlessly sweeping past stations where he wanted to, he had to, get off.

He woke sweating, panicked. He looked at his watch. Four-fifteen.

What if someone in a house on either side of the Devores' had, through a chink in the leaves, caught a glimpse of them under the arbor, in the dark garden, some prying pair of eyes.

"I saw these two carrying a woman wrapped in a blanket—I could swear one of them was the Devore boy—"

Impossible. Wasn't it?

What if the house on Morton Street was crawling with fuzz, looking for clues, dusting for fingerprints, waiting for a phone call?

Congratulations to us, Mouse had said. Everything was all right at this end. But how about the other end?

He had to know, had to have the reassurance of the telephone ringing there, and nobody, nobody at all, answering it.

If someone did answer, well— Hang up. Wrong number.

He went to the kitchen wall phone and dialed and got his father.

His heart gave one tremendous pound which interfered with his breathing. He had no idea later how he managed to produce the words he had repeated over and over to himself.

"Hi, Dad. We have Ma, we want two hundred and fifty thousand dollars for her . . ."

4

She did not scream upon waking up, or at any other time during her stay in the cellar. She had a feeling that once she started she might not be able to stop, and something as important as her life could come to a terrible end.

She opened her eyes at what she found to be seven-ten, if the round leather-cased clock a few feet away, on the step stool, was right. It probably was, it was ticking in a businesslike way.

Her head was heavy and her mouth dry. Her body felt as if made of lead.

She raised herself on one elbow and looked in utter disbelief at where, and how, she was. The bare overhead light bulb, the lack of daylight—conceivably it was morning but there was no morning here for her—increased her sense of an unlikely stage set, and she the unexplained lone actor in it.

A big high-ceilinged stone room, the shelves of empty wine racks as tall and neat as library stacks. An agreeable musty grapey memory of the contents of casks and bottles still in the air. The casks themselves, old, worn, handsome, lined up against the wall across from her.

For a sort of mental safety, for the moment, remain occupied with externals.

She studied the amenities provided for her on the step stool, opened one of the two thermos bottles and using the cup on top took a long drink of cold water.

Her suitcase, the lid propped up, was at the end of the mattress. She tried experimentally to get to her feet, found that her legs were unexpectedly weak, and put out a hand to support herself against the cool stone.

Her white nightgown was badly rumpled, and a vulnerable garment, which could be vaguely seen through.

Seated on the edge of the basket chair, she examined the contents of the suitcase that had been packed for her, by one of them.

Long pongee sashed robe, which she immediately put on. Three pairs of stretch lace pants, two bras, a pale blue slip, a yellow cashmere pullover, a long wraparound skirt of mattress ticking, a creamy sharkskin pants suit, two pairs of thin-strapped flat-heeled sandals, another nightgown; all packed, a bit helter-skelter, with obvious haste.

Was there any conclusion to be drawn about the length, or location, or purpose of her stay?

They, or the girl, must have done it while he was showing her over the house after her milk and his beer, Madeline busy in the kitchen. Or on the secret, previous visit, when Jane had met Mouse, or seen her.

She gave up her attempt to tiptoe around the unspeakable core without looking at it or touching it. Her head dropped into her hands.

The rank bitter coffee he'd been so obliging as to make, her sudden unusual overwhelming sleepiness, explained themselves with icy clarity. Up to a point.

And then the invading take-over hands, the girl sitting on her legs, Rob in his young power holding her flat, the prick of the needle on the inside of her elbow, and being wrapped, and carried, and removed, to whatever this place was, wherever it was.

Why?

Rebellion? Revenge? An elaborate prank, a punishment for

her? For being his parent, or on the girl's part anybody's mother?

Obviously not a wild, wicked impulse of the moment, a snatched chance. Care, thought, planning, shopping, had obviously gone into it.

The new muslin sheet, the thin blue synthetic blanket, the bloated yellow mattress, the gaily striped case of what might be considered under normal circumstances normal unimportant necessities—

Rob had, at home, a sumptuous sleeping bag from Bean in Maine, which would have done nicely.

Something obscenely unpleasant was to happen to her, but she was in the course of it to have her little comforts and niceties.

A sound escaped her, a long half moan, half wail, a sound of shock and inconsolable sorrow.

Rob. Robert Dermot Devore.

The noise she made came back at her from the stone walls and frightened her badly, which was in the long run helpful.

The thing to do was to be quiet about it, realistic, contained, keep your wits about you, shove emotion away, examine all this—what?—and deal with it.

They were two against one, and a great deal stronger than she was in some ways, but resources must and could be summoned. Not only for herself, but for Hugh. Her beloved Hugh. Solemn old-fashioned word; equally useful in thinking about a happy marriage of a close swift twenty years, or for cutting with a chisel into a gravestone. Madeline, beloved wife of . . . B. 1933. D. —?

Hugh . . . he was of course their victim, too. Whatever this was.

She found she had been weeping without knowing it, and took a handful of paper tissues from the box. Nose and cheeks and streaming eyes tidied, she went first to the door and tried the knob, and pushed, and pulled, although already she was quite sure she was locked in. Their, peculiar definition, prisoner.

With hands that steadied at desperate command, she opened the second thermos. Clear and very hot water, odorless when sniffed. Probably to make a cup of instant coffee with, but she didn't trust it.

There was a tentative noise at the door. She put a hand to her heart.

It opened and Rob came in, with Mouse. Mouse had a gun in her hand.

"Sit down, Ma, before you fall down," he said, trying, it seemed to her, for some kind of untenable lightness and casual cheer. She noticed that he didn't, or couldn't, look at her, but just past her, where the corner of an eye would do his examination for him.

Her eyes in disbelief on Mouse's gun—the girl shiningly washed and brushed, in the same jeans and pink shirt—she sat down.

"Rob," she said. "This is, you know—to borrow two words from you—absolutely mad. Whatever it's about."

"Funny, that's exactly what Dad said when I talked to him on the phone."

Somewhere in the back of her mind she had known. Known —*of course, what else?*—but rejected it because it was quite impossible.

You couldn't read the newspapers or look at a television screen or hear the radio without being aware of the incredible commonplaces: hijackings, kidnappings, abductions, hostages.

"He's back then . . ." Was it her voice?

"Yes, we just got out under the rope." There were bright red patches in his cheeks as though they were rouged and his eyes looked the way they did when he had had his childhood illnesses and was deep in fever.

"You stand right there, Mouse, okay? and I'll—" Watching her, he backed out of the room, bent down, and came in with a tray. It held a cup of coffee, a plate of toast, a glass of orange juice, a boiled egg in an eggcup, a gleaming thick damask napkin, heavy old-fashioned silver, and the kind of bell used for summoning servants. He set the tray on the card table.

Standing several feet away from her, looking down at the table, he said, "Might as well get it over with. Here's the deal. We're asking a certain sum of money, from him, for you. I can't believe he won't cough it up, and you know him, once he's going to do something he does it fast. It shouldn't be more than a few days . . . nobody's going to hurt you if you play along with us."

"Are there just the two of you or do I have other jailers, on whatever these premises are?" Her voice was still quiet.

"No, just us, Mouse and me."

"And the gun," Mouse said, speaking for the first time. "Which the way I figure it makes three of us. It's loaded, Mrs. Devore. It really is loaded."

"Ma doesn't have to be told anything twice," Rob said to her harshly.

"About this breakfast, and all your meals, you won't be drugged, this stuff is safe, and you really, you know, have to eat. It's only right to warn you not to start screaming, or try anything—not that it would do any good, there are six acres to this place. Whenever you want to use the bathroom"—he blushed—"for washing or showering or brushing your teeth or anything, ring the bell and Mouse will come down and take you up."

"Mouse and her companion, the one that makes three of you."

"Yes," Mouse said. She added idly, "Actually, there's a john down here, off the cook's rooms, but it has cockroaches or maggots or something in it and the tub is stained. Rob thought you wouldn't like it very much."

They left her to her breakfast. She heard the sound of a heavy bolt being shot into place as she picked up a piece of toast in hesitant fingers. Might as well go ahead and eat and drink, perhaps it didn't matter what the food did to her.

Perhaps nothing mattered.

She pulled herself back from this brink. No, have breakfast because it was the sensible thing to do, she would need her strength and her wits about her. The toast was hard to get down but the coffee was good and the egg fresh. Salt and pepper had been forgotten, but she ate the egg anyway, with determination.

The monogram on the silver was A. A for Aston? This was somebody's old and she suspected large house, from the size of the wine cellar. Somebody of substance, judging from the silver and the heavy damask napkin and the Sèvres porcelain plate and cup and saucer.

Certainly not her parents' house, unless they were away; but that would be too dangerous in any case, neighbors to see and report on the young comings and goings, possible summer droppers-in who hadn't heard that the Astons, senior, were off to Europe, or North East Harbor.

A relative? There was nothing to pin down about the initial A, they could have broken into any unoccupied but still furnished house that suited their purpose—isolated, lonely, soundproofed by the depth of surrounding acres.

She rang the bell vigorously and in under two minutes Mouse appeared. A frighteningly self-contained girl; she made no attempt at covering small talk as she conducted Madeline to the bathroom.

A long corridor, a laundry room, steep steps up to the kitchen door. The kitchen was starting on what she supposed would be a spectacular untidiness, beer cans and breakfast dishes, used pots and pans, crowding the counters and stove top.

She followed Mouse's straight back, her own as erect and braced. Through a large gloomy dining room with muffling dark green floor-length curtains closely drawn, vague shine of mahogany immensities, a cabbage-rosed carpet, dim and undistinguished oil painting of dead ducks and trout and rabbits, peaches and grapes. Into a broad deep hall where a great arched stained-glass window threw funereal reds and purples on the Persian rug, and on the massively newel-posted and banistered dark oak stairway.

The bathroom was to the left of the first landing, large and high-ceilinged, with a tub on legs and a mahogany-encased washstand. A gleaming new stall shower had been installed in a corner. The thick round glass racks held quantities of white bath and hand towels.

"Soap and everything's here, and—yes—you brought your case. I'll be right outside the door." Calm assurance; threat.

There was a large sash window beside the washstand. She went over to it and the first thing she saw, beyond the jut of the porch roof, was Rob, standing on the unkempt lawn in a brilliant swaying wash of sunlight and black shadow, his eyes on the window.

On guard.

She tried the old-fashioned latch arrangement, just in case. At some time, her warden out there might look the other way. The latch responded to her fingers. Bear it in mind. But remember, always remember, the gun in the hand of a girl who might not hesitate to use it. Perhaps not to kill, but to impede, cripple. A foot, an arm, a knee, a shoulder . . .

Weeping Norway spruces that must be ten stories high darkly embracing the house, glimpses of the corner of a barn, daisies in deep unmown grass, a stand of birches, a portion of a neglected herbaceous border in which tall pale blue iris and Oriental poppies bloomed defiantly—

All of this offered no clue as to where she was.

She could have no idea of the distance from New York because she'd been out, blanked, at whatever time they had gathered her up, transported her, and placed her on the mattress.

It could be anywhere in Connecticut, Massachusetts, New York, New Jersey, or points north and east.

The only thing she could clearly gather was that the owner of the house had let the lawns and gardens go, was not in residence, and perhaps—the obvious thing—had died, leaving behind him or her the ample Victorian house, for rent, furnished, or for sale.

She took care of the various needs of her body. There was hot water, in the shower stall; it must be an electric heater, the gas in an empty house would have been cut off. After she brushed her teeth, she looked at her face in the mirror. Eyes still bloodshot from crying. Faint freckles oddly prominent, greenish, or maybe it was the light cast by the spruces into this tall room. Before she composed, for herself, her features, she caught an eavesdropping impression of pain and staring unbelief.

She put on her robe and went over and said to the door, "Coming out now," not wanting to use the girl's name. There was a small bolt on the inside of the door she had tried, when entering, to push into place but thick layers of paint made it immovable, useless.

The door opened and she was conducted to her cellar, directed by Mouse to walk ahead of her. This basic security precaution had evidently not been thought of, on the way up.

Seated in the basket chair, she switched on the outer mind, which had nothing to do with emotion.

The money demand would be made and Hugh would meet it and she would be freed.

That, seen at its simplest and most comforting, was the shape of the immediate future.

But what about after the payment? It was a toss-up whether even infants, or young children incapable of clearly identifying their kidnappers, would be alive or dead following the delivery and pickup of ransom money.

One of her abductors was her own son. Was that some kind of guarantee of safety? Did he think it would be muffled, kept quiet, a family affair to be decently buried?

No, of course he—they—won't kill me. It would be too dangerous, too final, for him, that is.

If she was returned alive and it did leak out, the courts with luck on Rob's side might look on this as a nasty-normal '70's generation-gap prank, money handed back to his parents, everybody safe and well.

Gee, sorry, it was just, like, in fun, we wouldn't have hurt her, I have to admit I was kind of high, zonked, and didn't know what I was doing—

Perhaps a nominal sentence. Or perhaps no leak at all.

But if a body entered the matter, shot into eternity—

Hugh knows who has me, here. They'd look for him at once and for the rest of his life, and when they found him, as they would, there *went* the rest of his life.

His whole future caught, walled in, and dead in every sense that counted.

As dead as she was.

There was a beating in her throat as of a misplaced heart.

Nice well-brought-up affectionate boys—however undirected, restless, rebellious, at nineteen, however in thrall to girls giving off a scent of danger—don't kill their mothers.

Nor did they hold them for ransom, to their fathers.

If you wanted to be practical about your train of thought.

Oh, Hugh. Hugh, darling, do hurry up and get me out of this.

5

Devore stood watching the third-floor windows in the house at the back of his garden, willing the lights to come on. It was getting on for five-thirty. Walter Titus was an early riser.

He was a professor of history at Columbia, and a very old friend of Devore's. He had been recruited by the CIA five years before and had resigned in outrage at the death, in Chile, of Salvador Allende.

I don't have to tell you what will happen if you call in the police.

He knew that in his fury, and his terror, he couldn't handle it alone.

Titus might provide for the moment a safe and silent compromise.

When the brownstone on Murray Hill he had lived in for twenty years was set for attack by the wrecker's ball to make way for an apartment house, he remembered his friend's renovations in the Village and begged for accommodations there. Devore had been frantically busy at the time on the Talisman Foundation Tower, on East Forty-second Street, and as he often did fell back on the services of Madeline to get the interior of the third-floor apartment seen to. Titus wanted it furnished for him; he knew a great deal about history, and about the CIA, but nothing about how to buy a chair or table or mattress.

Madeline had set to work and after a few weeks the apartment looked, even though smelling of paint, as if it had always been there, over the garden, with its crewel-patterned linens and thin crisp striped chintz at the windows, its shelves waiting for his books, its benign cushiony comfort.

In the bedroom she had caused, for restfulness, floor and walls and ceiling to be painted a remote blue-gray, the lights came on.

Devore's hand went to the phone. "May I come over right away? Trouble."

"I'll put the coffee on, yes, come along."

Titus was tall, thin, stooped and gray, looking a good deal older than his fifty years, and his pince-nez did nothing to dispel this. The earnest if absentminded gaze, the vague high Bostonian voice were misleading; he was an acute man.

He stared at Devore and said, "Coffee first, for God's sake, man."

Devore accepted the cup, placed it carefully on the kitchen table, and told him, about Madeline.

The other man went to the window and looked across the garden to the Devore house.

"Rob," he said testingly. "Robert . . . and who do you suppose is 'we'?"

"On immediate instinct I'd say a girl, I don't know quite why." Devore tried to keep his voice level. "But there may be three, five, ten of them for all I know. A new game to play."

"Whiskey?"—anxiously.

"I've had a lot of it."

"Another won't hurt, in your coffee. I'll join you."

He poured generously and, pausing between cups, fingered his pince-nez back onto the high fine bridge of his nose.

"Is he, Rob . . . on things?"

"Marijuana, nothing else unless—" He shrugged. "I don't see a great deal of him anymore. And when I do see him we

don't exactly recognize each other. Now that you ask, *I've*
been on gin and a little vermouth, with an olive, for decades,
to say nothing of nicotine, no matter what fists they shake in
your face—"

"Drink your coffee. It's gone up God knows how much for
twelve ounces. Run through that phone call again?"

Devore did, and added, "This business of having a clear
view of the approach roads . . . it sounds like somewhere in
the country, and somewhere lonely, people living to the right
and left would wonder about a woman, screaming."

"Yes. Or it could be a simple bluff."

Devore considered this and then closed his mind to the picture of a prone body tied to some nearby city bed, the hell
with secrecy, seclusion, who needs it, with ropes and gags,
eyes staring and bulging, only the eyes able to move, to speak,
to beseech—

He put a hand to his own eyes and with a sideways brush of
the heel of his palm he removed the tears from his cheekbones.

"For sanity's sake, I'll stick to my private secret place in the
country," he said when he was able to talk. "She's not in
Greens Farms and if there is just the one other person involved, the girl, it could be a place connected with her, her
family. These things have to be planned in advance—you
don't just snatch a body and think, what on earth are we to do
with this?"

What had they done to her?

"I'm hungry and you need food." As English muffins were
toasted and eggs scrambled, Titus said, "Well. First, Jane.
Sisters see things and hear things. Then, his friends. If you
know who any of them are. Who's his girl now? Or who's he
been seeing most of lately, male or female? That lot, you
know, know all kinds of frightful things about each other and
think nothing of it."

In the end it was Devore who unwillingly but in deep need
ate most of the breakfast prepared by his host. Walter Titus

felt queasy himself. In his rusted bachelor way, he was a little in love with Madeline Devore.

He thought of her as being dressed always in white chiffon, and smelling of lilacs, although he supposed she occasionally shed her chiffon and her scent, and cooked things, and cleaned things, like other women.

"If across state lines, the FBI as well as the police," he ventured, a question in the form of a statement.

"No. Or, Christ, I don't know. For the moment you're my police and FBI. . . . They're men like any other men. Subject to ambition and impulses and personal drives. This is going to shape up as a nice big juicy story. Their names in the headlines. Their pictures on the television screen. Fame and fortune, promotion— Leaving all that aside, say that one man, or two, is disappointed in or enraged by his own kid—now go out and get this son of a bitch. The operation was successful but the patient—"

The unsaid word hung in silence, in the handsome blue and white kitchen.

Titus broke the silence. "Well, you've been given, excuse the expression, a period of grace to move around in. Until you get his instructions about the money." He went on delicately, "Speaking of that, I'm not as you know a rich man but I might be able to put my hands on twenty, twenty-five thousand—"

"No, but thanks. I've been working it out, over there"—nodding across at his vandalized house—"and I'll be able to do it."

"The business of knowing her kidnapper from—er—birth," his friend said gently. "And the aftermath . . . I think, you know, money delivered or not, we'd better try and find her."

"Yes," Devore said, his face clenched so that it was only decent to look away from it. "Yes, that's exactly—that's what I thought, too."

He went into the bathroom and was retchingly, violently ill. When he came back, he said, "We'll see. Maybe, a couple of hours from now, the police, I don't know . . ."

Titus was saddened to see him, this powerful and talented man, so in command of himself and his world, reduced momentarily to a smell of vomit and an uncertain, red-eyed mumbling.

"Let us simplify things," he said as if in his classroom. "There's another side to this coin. Kidnapping's not the nicest thing to do to one's mother but . . . death is something else, hers, that is. You pay the money, and off he goes. It's easy for them to drop out of the here and now, they do it all the time. Dye your hair, change your name, and if by any chance you want to work and make some money, borrow some idler's Social Security card. Or go to London, Tangiers, Afghanistan. Nothing to it. They all look so like each other—American vitamins, orthodontists, vats of milk and orange juice. And jeans are the greatest disguise ever invented."

"Yes, I'd gotten there before you," Devore said, his voice stronger now. "That's all very well when we speak of 'he.' But what about 'we'?"

Jane Devore at twelve had no problem with her parents. She was tolerantly fond of her mother, even though she didn't much resemble other people's mothers, and she adored her dark firm teasing father.

She was a strikingly beautiful, gifted, intelligent child. Her hair was a glistening red-struck deep brown, her eyes tilted a bit like her mother's but fiery brown and sparkling, her skin a thick soft magnolia white.

When handling one of Rob's tirades at the age of two, Devore said to Madeline, "I have bad news for you, you have given birth to my grandfather."

After Jane had turned from a prune into a baby, a girl, he said, "And here by God is my grandmother." She had been half Castilian, half Irish.

"You talk," Madeline said mildly, "as if I had no antecedents whatever."

She felt a little that way; a kind distant busy banker father thousands of miles away from her, while she was going to school in Rome, growing up. She often wondered then if, her birth having been the cause of her mother's death, he couldn't bear to have her in the same country with him.

And later found that this was all a matter of sad romantic imaginings, his two sisters had gone to the same convent, St. Lucy's, and had turned out quite well; and besides, his bank had a branch in Rome and he would unexpectedly descend upon the convent, to take her away for weekends, and for Christmas and Easter and summer holidays.

When Devore had asked her to marry him, or rather demanded it, she had said, "Well, yes, I'd love to, but I don't know how good I am, at families . . ."

On this June morning, Mrs. Boland waked Jane. She and Elizabeth had been up until three, talking and listening to records Jane had brought over with her, new sounds that puzzled and entranced them.

"They're my father's," Jane said. "They're called jazz."

Snatched upright from their twin beds, they rose and bent and whirled and danced to the odd beat, soar, gaiety.

"Won't your father mind, your taking his records like that?"

"No. He doesn't generally mind, about his things. I'll put them back in the morning."

The hand on her sleeping shoulder gave her a little shake. "Jane, for the third *time*—" She blinked and sat up, startled. "Your father called and wants you home, I suppose the two of you were up till all hours. Look at that log Elizabeth. Still asleep." Mrs. Boland, in nightgown and robe, was yawning herself.

It was seven o'clock. Jane was momentarily indignant; she never got up this early, not even during the school year. But it would be nice to see her father, after his week away in Japan. Funny he hadn't fallen straight into bed.

She retrieved her pink seersucker shorts and shirt from the floor and put them on, looked for her sandals and found them under Elizabeth's bed. It was okay to skip her teeth, seeing he was in such a hurry for her.

Suspecting that Mrs. Boland had gone back to catch up on her sleep, she ran down the stairs, through the living room and out into the brilliant morning. The fresh cool air smelled pleasant and poured over her skin like water, and it occurred to her that she might think about getting up early much more often. It was a private time, there weren't so many people.

Pale blue and white petunias bloomed in the white-painted wooden tubs on either side of the Devore front door. She had her hand on the knob when it opened, and she was hugged, and she knew immediately that something had happened, something bad.

He looked somehow awful, although he had obviously shaved and showered and his skin had a taut clean healthy gleam.

Devore had decided there wasn't any way he could keep it from her. Besides, he needed her help; and he thought she was old enough, and strong enough.

He told her in a few brief sentences what had happened.

It was ironic, he thought, that she had no trouble at all taking it in, her world was a tougher, more violent one than his had been at her age.

But she was at first indignant and then furious. "How absolutely unbelievably ghastly of him, the *nerve*—!"

He saw that it had not occurred to her yet to be frightened for her mother.

"Come get your breakfast and I'll have some more coffee with you. There are some things I want to ask you about."

"Anything, Daddy, anything at all."

She efficiently fried herself an egg, placed it on rye toast, and poured milk, while they talked.

"Rob over the phone used the word 'we,' so there's probably someone else—at least one other person—in this with him. Who's his girl? At the moment?"

In a kind of dream, he watched her pierce the egg yolk and spread it generously over the white.

"I don't know, I'm not sure, he switches around a lot, but the *last* girl I saw him with, he had her here, at the house . . . Let's see, was it last Thursday? Mother was out—"

"Kindly swallow. The day doesn't matter. What was she like?"

"He didn't bother to introduce me, I was in the dining room, on the window seat, reading, and come to think of it I'm not sure they knew I was there, the door was only half open. It was the last day of school and we got out early."

She hungrily consumed another mouthful. "He called her Mouse, crazy name. I took a peek around the door to see what would have a name like that. She's . . . funny." Searching for words, "Quiet, but—and dark, dark eyes, dark hair, dark"— more fumbling—"just *dark* . . ." She fingered her own hair. "I know I am too but she's different."

"What about his friends, boys, are they around?"

"*You* remember. Batty, and Lee and John Tanager are all in Europe. That fight when you told him he couldn't go after all . . ."

Rob was to have had a backpacking summer abroad, which had been abruptly and summarily canceled when he dropped out of college.

Returning to the girl, Jane said, "They were sitting on the sofa, he had his arm around her and he was kissing her, so he must like her. It was all right, they had their clothes on and everything."

"Under the circumstances, there wouldn't have been a great deal in the way of conversation?"

"You sound as if your throat's sore, should you have aspirin? . . . No, not much for a while and then she said, 'Stop, because we've got to talk and we're getting nowhere fast.'"

Devore's breathing stilled for a moment. "And then what?"

"I was reading, I was only half listening, they were boring—"

"It's important, Jane."

Jane finished her milk, her eyes squinting into the near distance with the effort of memory.

"Something about a house, her aunt's house, the aunt was dead and there was no one in it—"

"And what else?"

His voice made her jump. For a second or two she was terrified at the expression on his face, and he was a color she'd never seen on him before, sort of blue.

She put her face into her cupped hands and closed her eyes hard. "I don't know," she said in a muffled voice, "if there's any more that I heard, that they said—"

"Try, Jane, for Christ's sake try." He never swore in front of her. Very deliberately, he added, "It might mean your mother's life."

It couldn't, he immediately realized, have been a greater mistake, urgently as it needed to be said.

She stared at him, her mind a sudden blank, her skin shocked colorless, and then her imagination leaped on the words. She burst into a storm of tears and ran in terror to his arms.

6

Al Madonna flew east on TWA. He had just completed, with an associate in Detroit, a complicated but highly profitable sale of arms to Lebanon. He was now interested in seeing what the horse he owned, a horse named Daybreak, might promise to do at the Monmouth Park race meeting.

He was in his middle twenties. He had sunburned pitted skin, tightly curling black hair, laughing burning eyes under heavy lids, a snub face, a hoarse husky voice considered by his girls to be sexy. He was neither short nor tall but his shoulders were powerful; he rolled and swaggered a little as he walked, like a sailor. He exuded an animal energy.

"I don't think he's Mafia," Mouse had once said of him to Rob, "but a kind of gang mostly by himself."

Feeling pleasantly rich as he did, and wanting to celebrate, just any of his girls didn't suit him: he wanted Mouse.

He'd only known her for a few months but she'd gotten to him. There was nothing, for kicks, she wouldn't do.

Which was made even more intriguing by her clean schoolroom looks, scrubbed skin, shining hair, and her immaculate rich-girl diction when she chose to use it.

He called her apartment on Leroy Street and got one of her roommates, Evelyn something.

"Mouse hasn't been around since yesterday. Any message?"

Well, naturally he didn't expect a girl like her to retire to a nunnery when he had to leave town on business. But now that he was back—

A challenge. Al Madonna enjoyed challenges. "Who's she been seeing? Lately."

"His name is Rob, Devore, I think."

Al remembered him from the party, in May. Looking like something out of the goddam Round Table or whatever it was, or a Crusader, with his long shining blond hair. But a kid, just a kid, couldn't have hit twenty yet.

He went through the telephone book and found a number of Devores, including Devore Associates on Fifty-eighth Street. With a huntsman's relish, he called them all.

If Mouse was off and away with someone, in town or out, you could be sure it wasn't with a girl friend of hers.

He used the same question every time the phone was picked up. "Is Rob there, please?"

A man answered when he dialed an H. L. Devore, Morton Street. Funny voice, deep, raw-edged, as though he'd been drinking or up all night.

"Is Rob there, please?"

"No, not at the moment—who's this?" Something about the way it was asked made Al interested, very.

"A friend, Mike Finch," he invented instantly. "I'm trying to track down another friend, as a matter of fact, a girl named Margaret, though they call her Mouse."

The voice said slowly, carefully, "Mouse? Oh yes, Mouse . . . let's see now . . . what's her last name again?"

Al didn't like the needling intensity he felt at the other end of the line.

Instinctive deviousness provided the answer. "Smith." As if there could be two of anything named Mouse—

"And where does she live when you're not looking for her at this number?"

He didn't like that question either. Maybe Mouse had really

pulled something, screwed these Devores up in some way, in particular the blondie-boy son.

"Feel free to use the phone book," he said, and hung up.

Jane had been listening, directed by a hurry-up gesturing hand, on the library extension.

"No, I don't know his voice. I don't like the way he sounds."

So, big deal, Rob Devore wasn't there, Al thought. Then why had the strong and somehow authoritative voice sounded, well, call it a little terrified?

Parents these days terrified easy, he told himself with an inward grin. Still interesting, though, to chew around the edges of, turn over in his mind. I smell Mouse, he said.

At a little after eight, Jane, rising to her new responsibilities, said, "Shouldn't you go to bed, Daddy, for a few hours at least?" She added in a practical fashion, "You'll have to be on your toes, and right now you look awful. I won't make any calls out and if the phone rings—if it's anyone who—of course I'll wake you right up."

Her tears had been washed away and because it was unthinkable she had also temporarily cleansed from her mind the idea that her brother would do anything really awful to her mother.

Devore, whose eyes felt as if they were burning holes in his head and whose brain seemed suddenly not to want to function, reluctantly agreed. After he had smoothed over the distressed toss of the striped sheet—*what had they done to her here?*—he went to the window and looked out.

It would be nice if none of it was true, a crude, cruel joke on Rob's part. Knowing that for some reason his mother wouldn't be home and saying, I'll show *him*.

If that were so, he might any second now see Madeline coming around the angle of Morton Street, on the sidewalk, the sun on her pale red-fair hair.

He wrote explanatory lines for her to speak when she finally came in at the door.

"Hugh, I'm so sorry, I had a brandy too many and fell asleep at—"

No.

"I went to an opening and on to a party and they wanted to drive to Dobbs Ferry afterward and go swimming in their pool—"

No.

And again, "I can hardly bear to tell you, Hugh, but there is this . . . it's happened . . . I love him . . . there's nothing I can do about it . . ."

No.

Undressing, he worried about Titus, who had promised to do nothing about the police until Devore made up his mind one way or the other. But what if he went ahead anyway?

Somebody's conniving eyes watching the Devore house, seeing the police car drive up to the door, a phone call to nowhere, where Madeline was . . .

"That wraps it up, he's just called in the police."

He dismissed it; you couldn't get safely from one minute to the next one, thinking in this way. Fighting sleep, which was clutching at him, ready to topple on him, he thought wearily, Funny, I have always been fond of, loved Jane, but I had no idea what a good staunch girl she is.

Jane sat where she had been curled Thursday of last week, on the flowered linen window seat in the dining room. She held the same book she had been reading, *Dracula,* but she made no attempt to read it now.

She was scouring her mind as she had never before tried to do, searching in every corner of it and behind every door.

It had been about two o'clock in the afternoon, a time of day when sunlight fell on the lacquered white of the oval dining table by the window and made a dazzle of it, and rioted in the hanging baskets in the long windows beyond it, immense Boston ferns, caladium, lantana.

There had been a smell of cinnamon in the air, something

her mother had cooked before she left the house. And the voices from the next room, long silences, and then talking again . . .

". . . my aunt's house, she's dead and there's no one in it . . ."

"Great, where is it?"

"It's in . . ."

I'm getting warmer, Jane thought, excited. I'm reconstructing a crime, that's what I'm doing.

Down deeper, now, for the name of the town. It had almost disappeared under a sudden furious argument of automobile horns in Morton Street, but if she worked at it— People could hear a lot of sounds at once if they were New York-trained.

It had something, she thought, to do with virtue, or being good, or wise. But she wasn't even sure of that; she had come to a marvelously scary place in her book and had only been listening with one ear, idly.

People making love to each other were boring, especially if they were in your own family.

Purity? No. Chastity? Not that either. Thrift? Hopeless, and now she was getting farther away from it, getting cold again. Perhaps it would be wise to drop it for the moment and then it might come suddenly out of nowhere and whack her in the head, as elusive bits and pieces of memory often did.

And she could cry in triumph to her father, "I know the town, I know where she is, and now we can go there and get her—"

Like most intelligent, civilized people, Madeline Devore had her occasional moments of self-questioning, self-doubt.

She sat in the basket chair, bent into herself, hands desperately holding on to each other until she noticed it and loosened them, and thought, Where did I go wrong? What did I do or not do, that this impossible, this in a way ludicrous, thing could happen to me, and to Hugh?

And then, mutinous idea, strong and fresh as a salt breeze: Where did *he* go wrong?

She had always thought that Rob, without being demonstrative about it, was fond of her. He liked to tease her; and in turn, she sometimes said things that made him laugh, with her and not at her. There were inevitable clashes with his father, but it wouldn't be normal if there weren't.

"In any place but this benighted country, where adolescence is allowed to drag on until at least thirty, he'd be a grown man," Hugh said. "You may not be aware of it, but he's competing, with me, for you."

Allow herself a long breath. Lean back. What would she have been doing at home this morning? Taking the dinner dishes out of the dishwasher and putting them away, putting the breakfast dishes in, summoning Jane from the Bolands' if it got to be after ten, and beginning to wait with pleasure for Hugh.

After her scanty housekeeping here in her cellar was attended to, she dressed, in her creamy pants suit because there was a chill in the air, a chill of moist old stone, and she wanted her legs covered, and her arms. She placed the easeled round mirror on the table and was sitting doing her hair when the door opened and Rob came in.

He stopped just inside, for a moment pierced by the graceful domestic womanly gestures, the long hands twisting the pale gleaming hair into its small high chignon, thrusting a few tortoise pins invisibly in.

He was breaking his own rules, and Mouse's, but he wanted to say or do something, convey something, to get that look of stunned suffering out of her pale hazel eyes.

"Where's your chum?" The faint whip in her voice brought a bright pink to his face.

"Look, Ma, there's nothing personal in this . . ."

"Nothing personal?" she interrupted. "Then who am I, Rob?"

"I mean, there's nothing against *you*, it's strictly"—he

paused and brought out the words, which fell crazily on his own ears—"a financial matter."

He had no intention of telling her the price they had put upon her; that would be going too far and it might give her something else to worry about, ruining the old man.

Madeline finished her hair and said as though to herself, "Your father . . ."

What was he thinking, feeling now? She knew that she was alive, but he couldn't know that. Her heart began to pound savagely and nausea rose in her.

Hugh, stripped and frantic. His wife. His son.

Hugh, doubly destroyed.

She was unable to look at Rob, standing by the door, meet his eyes. Who *is* Rob?

Or was it the girl? You couldn't hold her singly responsible, but—

Something in her chemistry kindling a like substance, unseen, hidden, in his? She had felt Rob's fascination with her, at dinner and over the calamitous coffee. Like a strong dark current flowing from him to her, his radiant eyes seldom removed from her face, her body. She couldn't say now whether it was a two-way current. Mouse Aston had been so—not quiet, the word suggested repose—so silent, so ungivingly cool.

Up to a little while ago, she had had an idea that the whole stage set might fall apart, game over, all the juice squeezed out of the ridiculous joke.

"Okay, Ma, forget it—I've given *him* a scare all right. Now we'll drive you home."

He would have arrived back from whatever emotional island he had landed on, see light, see sense. See what he had been thinking of doing, the enormity of it, and pulled swiftly and healthily back.

As she thought about using her new lipstick and decided against it, the comforting idea of the bad, black joke slowly but convincingly died.

"By any chance did you bring along my pocketbook?"

He leaped at the break in her silence. "No, there's your checkbook and you said you always kept a fifty-dollar bill hidden in it somewhere because of that time you were stranded in Dallas—"

Her voice changed. It was clear, soft, and direct.

"Rob, had you ever really thought, dreamed, that you could get away with this nonsense?"

He wished now he hadn't come down to the cellar. He said, the words pulled out of him, "You wouldn't put me in prison for the rest of my life, would you? Or—they're getting very big now on capital punishment, maybe I'd be in time for that. It's only money, Ma. *You* always said money wasn't all that important, other things came before it."

"And what," she asked, her voice delicately walking on eggs, "had you planned to do, afterward?"

"If it goes all right, and I don't see why it shouldn't, just plain cut out, off and away, never mind where, new name, new everything, everybody safe and sound."

She looked at him with eyes that made him move his gaze to the stone wall beyond her head.

"Safe and sound? In a way, there will be a kind of death involved, for three people. Yes, you too."

He studied with what seemed to be great interest the corner strolling of a spider on the ceiling.

"I'm not threatening you," she said. "I'm just telling you, this is the deciding action of your life. *Your* life. It will dictate the rest of it."

He was for a moment back in extreme youth and a long firm soft hand was pulling him away from danger, a tree branch that wouldn't even hold his featherweight, a heavy sucking swell of sea at an innocent golden edge of sand.

She thought she could see at least part of the way into his mind. The first winy excitement over, the cloak-and-dagger dash through the night with the blanketed body, the successful reaching of wherever they were, the sheer impossible nerve of it. Mission accomplished. Live television.

Then the inevitable physical and emotional letdown, the long held breath expelled. The hard part was beginning now, the waiting, the watching, the listening. The wondering. Police? FBI? Guns being trained on the house from distant unseen trees? An innocent-looking helicopter or private pleasure plane skimming about in the summer skies? The sound of a passing car on some nearby road, braking; or turning on its siren.

And maybe—just maybe—getting an inkling of the true size and shape of what he was doing to his mother and father. And to himself.

She got up from her chair and went over to him. She was just three or four inches shorter than he, an erect slender woman. She sent everything of herself across the foot or so that separated them.

"Rob—"

He backed away a little.

"Suppose we wind this thing up, right now? Undo it, forget it. Take me home. I promise you solemnly, for myself and for your father, that nothing will be done about it, absolutely nothing."

Nothing that hadn't, inerasably, been done already.

He hesitated. She had no way of knowing whether he was framing a tough answer, or was about to capitulate, when the door was flung open, crashing into his back, and Mouse came furiously in with her gun.

"It's too late," Rob said, harshly and defensively, to both of them.

"Yes, whatever it is you asked him to do, it's too late, Mrs. Devore," Mouse said.

One-handedly, she hurled Rob around by a shoulder so that he stood facing her at Madeline's side. There were tears of rage in her dark eyes.

"What the hell is this, Rob? You promised. Everything. Together."

"I just wanted to see if she was okay," Rob said neutrally.

"Nobody's going to be okay if we don't stick to the rules," Mouse said. "Was Mother's little boy thinking about leading Mother by the hand out of here, and kissing her goodbye at the gates, and telling her it was, like, all in fun?"

Rob reached out and snatched the gun from her.

"I'll hold this for a while, seeing the state you're in."

Clever Mouse, Madeline thought bitterly.

Challenging his manhood.

Rob held the gun as though he had somehow or other laid a palm on a rattlesnake's head. Then his grip on it tightened and he smiled at Mouse.

"Like you said, including this thing. Everything. Together."

7

The real estate agency had advertised the house in five newspapers, including the New York *Times*, as: "Delightful country residence, set in 6 acres. 10 rms., 3 bed, 4 bath, 2 useful
outbuildings, gardens, brook, woodland, lily pond. For sale or
rent, furnished or unfurnished. Privacy guaranteed."

The ad had run on and off since February, but so far there
were no takers.

Mr. and Mrs. Thomas McIntosh, rich and in their late six-
ties, were interested in a house where they could spend the six
months left over from their place in Key West. "A pretty
house," Mrs. McIntosh specified to the real estate agent, Mr.
Cove. "A cool situation. Easy to care for, I don't know what's
come over people, they don't want to be servants any more.
We've only our Bessie."

"I have just the thing for you," said Mr. Cove.

She was daunted, even before seeing the delightful residence, by the length of the drive, the looming of the rhododendrons with beyond them the great dark spruces.

Mr. Cove's Ford rounded a final curve and the house presented itself to her apprehensive eyes, porches and cupolas
seeming to multiply.

Before they got out of the car, she whispered to Mr.

McIntosh, "Father, it's too large, much too large, I couldn't possibly—even with help—"

"Yes, Mother, but let's look it over. Who knows?" Mr. McIntosh adored wandering through other people's houses, a form of allowable prying. It was even better when they were furnished.

Mr. Cove in the front seat had wilted at her whisper and cheered up at his.

"Fine old place," he said as they went up the front porch stairs. "You don't find this kind of roomy house anymore, they don't build them this way, can't afford to, I suppose."

He inserted his key and as always had a little struggle with the cranky lock. To cover this, he said, getting the door open in midsentence, "It was owned by a very old lady and as you'll see she kept it in perfect—"

From the living room to the right of the hall a voice said, "I swear to God you're cheating."

Mr. Cove, bathed in reds and purples from the stained-glass window, said, "Oh, dear me."

They were sitting at the round table draped to the floor in maroon velvet edged with bullion fringe, playing poker.

Apart from his illicit three-hour sleep in the kitchen, Rob had not yet had his spell in bed. Funny feeling, but he didn't right now want to leave Mouse, alone, with the gun, in charge of his mother.

Anyone got fed up with their parents, what else, but the way she talked about hers chilled him.

He wouldn't like Mouse to get the idea that Madeline Devore was a kind of stand-in for her own mother.

On his insistence, the gun was now placed on a corner of the kitchen counter, so that it was theoretically available to him, too, when he was on guard.

" . . . she kept it in perfect . . ."

Mouse's indrawn hissing breath sounded as though someone had just stepped on her foot. Rob merely stared at the three people in the living-room doorway, an elderly man and woman and a little plump second man with an air of bustle.

"I demand to know who you are," the plump man said, bristling. "This house is vacant. I am Edward Cove of Cove and Sniffen Real Estate. Who are you and what are you doing here?"

Mouse saw from Rob's eyes that he was in a silent panic. Her own reactions, responses, worked like lightning.

"This is my aunt's house," she said, underlining it by adding, "I'm her niece. My friend and I are having a day here, I wanted him to see Aunt Grace's place. Great-aunt really, but she didn't like it because it made her sound so old."

Mr. McIntosh thought the handsome boy looked ill, white under his warm golden sun coloring. Maybe a—hashish picnic or something, he thought, disapproving and vicariously thrilled.

"I demand to see identification," Mr. Cove said.

"Demand, demand." Mouse got up and went to the door. Her shoulder bag was hung over the knob. She flipped photographs and credit card windows in her wallet, to her driver's license, and showed it to him. Margaret Aston. Description, age, address.

Later, Rob said, "Are you *crazy*? That license, on a silver platter—"

"Are *you* crazy? How do you know he wouldn't have gone straight to the police station and said there were squatters here on this valuable private property. In this town if you own a house and land you're, like, God. You wouldn't have wanted a houseful of fuzz, would you?"

Convinced but nevertheless nettled, Mr. Cove said, "Well, all right, I'm going to show my clients through." He hoped they hadn't made a mess of the place already.

Mouse went back and sat down. Under the shield of the velvet table cover she kicked Rob, hard.

"Your beer ought to be cold by now. And I'm dying of thirst, bring me one."

He stared at her and then understood. For a short time his brain had felt stopped, nothing in it but icy fear, all thought suspended.

The gun, on the kitchen counter. Women always took a great interest in kitchens.

"Well, as you see, the living room," Mr. Cove was saying. "Very commodious, and it's only those long heavy curtains— but the best-quality silk brocade—that make it look dark, it faces east, should get cheerful morning sun . . ."

Rob walked rapidly past them, through the dining room and into the kitchen. Where the hell could he put the gun? It would show as a bulge in his pocket. If he put it in a cabinet or drawer the woman might poke about, open things to see if there was room for all her stuff—

But there wasn't time. He got up on a kitchen chair and put it on top of the high white wall-hung cabinet, at the back.

What if the bell rang, from the cellar?

Mouse never drank beer but he got out an extra can for her anyway and saw that his hands were shaking. His hands had never before in his life shaken.

This wouldn't do at all. Cool it. Mouse so on top of everything. Kicking him, just in time. His shin still hurt.

The wine cellar was, let's see, at a rough guess underneath the living room.

What if she heard tramping sounds from above? One short round man, one tall large man, one dumpy high-heeled woman? In an old place like this, the floors were probably too thick—

Or were they?

Would she, in hope and panic, seize her bell and ring and ring and ring it?

Or maybe she'd be cowering, as he was now, her heartbeat hurting her—

"Are there just the two of you or do I have other jailers, on whatever these premises are?"

He went with the two cans of beer back into the living

room. Mouse opened hers, took a small sip, made a face, and put it down on the table, where the act would be immortalized by a crisp dried dark ring on the red velvet.

Heading back for his position of commander, not follower, Rob said, voice low, "I still worry about that license. Why didn't you just say you were her niece but give another name? Now, on the books, Margaret Aston is in this house at ten-fifty A.M. on June eleventh—"

"Don't forget," Mouse said, "that after this we won't be us anymore."

The murmured words pierced him.

We won't be us anymore.

New names, dyes, disguises, the dark glasses, the freckles Mouse had amused herself practicing applying last week. "I'll be blond, raggedy short blond," she had said. "I like *you* blond, but you'd look terrific with dark hair, of course you'll have to wear it some other way." In the planning, it had sounded like crazy nose-thumbing fun.

Rob, Rob Devore, Robert Dermot Devore, in a way a body, extinct, to be left behind at this house in Prudence, New Jersey.

He never forgot that white thunderstruck moment of realization. He remembered everything about it, the musty smell in the living room, the slow explosion of a large bubble on top of Mouse's beer can, the dazzling bar of sunlight on the floor along the bottom of the heavy dark red curtains, the sound of feet trudging up the stairway, Mr. Cove's voice, "Wait till you see the size of the bedrooms . . ."

He cherished himself, everything about himself.

And here he was set about losing himself, forever.

"In a way, there will be a kind of death involved, for three people. Yes, you too."

He was aware of Mouse, staring at him, staring into him, as though she had burrowed herself inside his head.

"You don't get any gold stars for this morning," she muttered severely. "My hero—look at you. Green." Uncannily, she found a knife to turn in the wound. "Remember you said when I first talked to you about it you'd thought it up the day before? And you were going to ask me to help."

"Yes, I know." He took a gulp of beer and choked on it and thought for a moment he would throw up, right there. Deep breathing was supposed to help. He tried it, and it did.

Sick stomach and trembling hands—who was this person Rob?

Her muttering turned brisk. "When we hear them coming down the stairs, go into the kitchen, or better still go now, they might use the back stairs. Lean against the kitchen door so they won't see the missing pane, it's kind of a giveaway. Put a big pot of water on to heat so it looks like you have a reason to be standing around, waiting."

Any kind of action would be better than sitting thinking about the end of himself.

And of course, what he had been worrying about wouldn't happen after all if something slipped, with these people here.

If, say, she began to ring her bell. It could be heard clearly from the kitchen. Even if she didn't connect overhead footsteps with innocent strangers she might, plain, have to go to the bathroom.

Or if the couple were pleased by the house, wanted to move in right away, get out of some motel or hotel they'd been staying in, after all the place was furnished and ready—

Was he half hoping—crazy—that someone would stop this express train and they'd all three of them get off? Before it was too late?

He concluded that for the moment it was wiser not to think at all right now, about anything. Just act.

From open shelves of utensils, he took a big aluminum soup pot, filled it with water, and switched on the large burner under it. He went and leaned against the door.

Following orders again, he told himself, but of course he should have thought if it first. After a few minutes, feet began to descend the boxed-in back staircase to the kitchen. Okay, Mouse, right again.

" . . . well, yes, but I'm afraid it's much too large," the woman's voice said. "Don't you think so, Father?" her voice appealing for a decisive male refusal, from him.

Thank God *his* mother never called his father Father.

"Whatever you think, Mother," Mr. McIntosh said, handing the decision back to her. They emerged into the kitchen and Mr. Cove made a small clucking noise at the disorder of it. He hadn't quite given up.

"This kitchen's a prize," he said. "Twenty by twenty feet. New stove put in last year and, as you see, two refrigerators."

Mrs. McIntosh looked at Rob, braced against the door, hands in his pockets. A shame, really, that boy having to see to whatever he was cooking, with that girl lounging around in the living room. That girl entered the kitchen and got herself a glass of milk and sat down at the table with it.

Well, guts, Rob said grudgingly to himself. He was glad of her company.

Mr. Cove sighed at Mrs. McIntosh's lack of response to the kitchen.

Rob was listening for the bell so hard that he heard it in his head, and started, and they all stared at him.

"Well, there you have it," Mr. Cove said. "Extensive cellars, of course, sometimes the man of the house is interested in the cellars."

Mr. McIntosh did look interested. "None of your gaping hole in the ground, underneath here," Mr. Cove went on doggedly, stamping his foot on the dark green asphalt tile of the kitchen floor. "Laundry room, cook's quarters, storerooms—with shelves, very deep shelves—and a wine cellar fit for a . . . a nobleman," he brought out triumphantly.

"And," Mouse said, milk on her upper lip, "rats. Like, hundreds of them. I started down to look for an old photograph album, in the storeroom, in a trunk. I was never so scared in all my life."

Mr. Cove glared at her and Mr. McIntosh looked at the

white paneled door as though an inundation of rats might any minute claw it open. He said hastily, "For the time being I'll take your word for the cellars."

"Of course, they could be dealt with, the work of an hour or so if you—"

He felt a wall of resistance coming at him and made one last try, moving toward the kitchen door. "Let's take a quick look at the outbuildings. A four-car garage with an apartment over it—I don't know if you keep a chauffeur—and then there's a . . ."

Mrs. McIntosh took the coward's way out. "My feet hurt, Father, and I don't feel at all well. Thank you so much, Mr. Cove, we must be going, we'll think about it. Even though it's too large, much too large. We'll let you know by telephone, today or tomorrow . . ."

Departing with them, toward the front door, Mr. Cove favored Mouse with a second glare. That one, with her rats—there might have been one thin thread of a chance, but now—

She had sent him and his commission right straight down the drain.

All the same, he'd better have the cellar seen to, and the sooner, the better.

8

Walter Titus had an appointment at ten o'clock at his dentist's in Rockefeller Center. He dazedly kept it and it was only when he was in the chair, and the needle had been inserted in his upper right gum and the root-canal work begun, that he thought, What the hell am I doing here?

Too late to jump up and run. The root-canal work proceeded. He could swear he felt distant pain through the anesthetic. Hands damp and gripping the arms of the long reclining chair, he devoted himself to enduring this, getting through it, it couldn't take forever.

Where was Madeline? What was she thinking, feeling? Was she weeping in anguish, or blue with fear, were her freckles standing out in that way they did when she was very tired?

To him, she was one of the few originals around, but to be fair, so was her husband.

A mixture, worldly and shy, kind, amused, reserved; her own private warmths, confidences, passions, quietly contained behind the pale hazel eyes, the cupped high forehead.

He knew she had a swift keen intelligence and an uncanny awareness of other people. And she had in abundance that elusive lovely quality, charm.

She had once, late, at a party when he was murmuring well-scotched compliments to her, explained that to him. Or so she thought.

Charm, she told him, is what happens when in a way you're afraid of everyone so you learn how to please. Charm is meeting someone—or no one who matters but it becomes a habit—and saying to yourself, "In what manner can I protect myself from you? And/or be liked, approved by you?" Charm is singing for your supper without being caught doing it.

"You sound like a willow being worried about the noise the wind makes of you when it blows through," Titus said, feeling lyrical if a bit blurred. "However, you may have a point," thinking about putting his arm around her shoulders but changing his mind when Devore came into the kitchen to get people drinks. "But you're stuck with it, all of it, Madeline."

Released from the long chair after an hour, he took a cab downtown to his apartment, changed out of his dentist's-appointment gray suit into corduroys and a favorite shabby blue shirt with a frayed collar, and went down to the ground floor in the small silkily moving elevator. Fortunately he had no classes today.

Not that he would have gone in if he had.

He went out his front door, turned left, and entered the garage, to which he had a key because his storage cupboards were there. Rob's car glimmered red beside his father's Mercedes. They must have used the girl's car, if Devore was right and it was a girl. Or a car she had borrowed from someone else. They shared things. Not, in some ways, any longer possessive.

Yes, he thought, standing in the garage, very neat, it couldn't have been set up any better for them. A car pulled in here, invisible from the street, waiting. The long thick grape arbor he now entered, leading from the Devore house to the garage, thick obscuring leaves to hide them, with what they were carrying, or dragging along.

He paused on the back step to look over the garden, marveling at the misleading peace it suggested on this bright blue morning. Not a whisper of disaster in the sunny air.

Madeline's feathery tall cosmos already blossoming lavender and white and black-red. Lacy white wrought-iron furniture set on a circle of white-painted brick, white hanging baskets of blue and purple petunias on the garden walls. Tubs of white geraniums, a great tall ash tree shaking shadow over the whole. It was her particular place; he saw her there as he had seen her from his window yesterday, weeding the cosmos and then cutting petunias and yellow roses.

He hesitated a little before lightly pressing the bell. But Devore wouldn't have come to him if he wanted to handle it alone. He saw his powerful capable friend as a sort of prone Gulliver attacked by contemporary infants.

The door was opened instantly by Jane. He saw that she had been crying but she projected an air of competence.

"Where's your father?"

"Asleep," Jane said.

"*Asleep!*" Titus was scandalized.

"Yes, he'd had it. He can't sleep much, on planes. I mean," defendingly, "all the way here from Tokyo . . . And he knew he's going to need sort of, everything he's got before he—before they—"

She broke off. If you put it into words, it made itself real again, filling the kitchen, filling the house, making the walls explode.

"No call, no word yet?"

"No. He told Daddy he wouldn't be using the phone to tell him about the arrangements, but that," Jane said keenly, "could have been just talk, so that there wouldn't be a tape or something hooked to the phone. By the police, or someone."

Taken aback, Titus reminded himself that television children knew about the *i*-dotting and *t*-crossing of crime.

"I'll have a look at Rob's room if I may," he said.

"Yes, go ahead. I looked around but you'd know what to look for and I didn't . . ."

Rob was now—what?—a criminal, his things to be examined, and her mother was not there to be consulted, and she was the only one awake in the house. Sustained by company, she went up the stairs with her father's friend. Devore's door was open. Titus saw the long sleeping figure and heard the profound silence but to him the bedroom seemed to be beating, like a heart.

Rob's room was, for his age and sex, tidy. Either domestic discipline, Titus thought, or that competent cleaning woman of theirs, lent to him once a week.

A large willow hamper of records at the end of the brass bed, expensive stereo equipment on the deep windowsill, closet door open showing a jam of colorful clothing. He tried to remember if he had ever considered Rob Devore spoiled, his every want foreseen and attended to lavishly, like others of his generation; and on the whole he didn't think so, that wasn't the Devores' way with their children. Of course, Devore made a great deal of money, and had done so since his brilliant early start, and money produced Things, quantities of them.

In spite of Jane's endorsement, he had no idea of what he was looking for. Perhaps something scrawled hastily on a piece of paper as an aid to memory, then overlooked, forgotten—a name, a route number, a notation of time, or place—

His patient thorough search went unrewarded. Panic suddenly squeezed him. Devore asleep, and the minutes, the lethal, loaded minutes ticking away.

He decided that, hell or high water, Devore or no Devore, if nothing at all had happened by one o'clock at the latest, he would notify the police and the FBI.

Devore woke at a little before noon. There was no merciful easing into consciousness. It crashed immediately and abruptly over him, a fist that had been waiting above his head until at last he opened his eyes.

He made an inarticulate noise, a half groan, caught it back, and got up and dressed.

Titus was waiting for him in the living room, prowling from one end of it to the other in his stooped way.

As though picking up a conversation just left off, he said, "Has Rob ever been arrested for anything? Traffic violation, something like that? Possession of drugs?"

"You mean," Devore said, "so that they'd have his prints on file—no. Never. Or not that I know of." Titus was relieved to hear the resonant strength back in his voice. "And what good are fingerprints anyway when you don't know where the fingers are?"

"Well, prints, yes, but I was wondering if he'd shown any tendency to—I mean, are there any family secrets about him, things he's done, that you've very naturally kept to yourself?"

"No. Apart from what *he* may have kept to himself. He seemed maddeningly normal—predictable—for his age and time, if you follow me."

"You know what you're going to have to do, like it or not. Or if you don't I will. How would you like having to tell yourself the rest of your life that it was your fault, what happened to her, because you wouldn't call in the obvious help?"

"Yes, *yes*, maybe a little later," Devore said with an enraged and frustrated shake of his head. "For Christ's sake let's take this minute by minute, not go leaping ahead, or we'll both go mad."

Why, he asked himself, did he keep expecting that Rob would lose his nerve, get a sudden glimpse of perhaps disastrous consequences waiting for him, and wake up to sanity of a kind? And then there would be the voice on the phone, his or Madeline's, stop worrying, joke over. And she would be on her way back.

Yes, why? He had no longer any reason to trust in Rob's eventual good faith; and the girl, or the boy, or boys, whoever it was with him—"we"—might have fears and second thoughts of their own.

Hey, but she knows us now—

And, back to Rob, once you started on the greased slide, down into calculated, deliberate danger, there might be no handhold and no way to stop yourself even if you wanted to.

He became aware of Titus's voice.

"It's minute to minute *I'm* thinking about." Titus, not liking the way he sounded, shrill, looked at his watch and added more calmly, "We have arrived at an entirely respectable hour for a drink. I'll go and get it."

The telephone on the long low bookshelf across the room rang. Devore walked to it rigidly erect.

"Oh, it's you, Hugh," Pamela Broderick said. "Madeline there?"

Careful. Shut up. "No, not right now." He didn't trust himself to idle covering talk.

"Nice trip to Japan? Hail the conquering hero and everything. I'm just in from Fire Island. Ghastly traffic. We want you for dinner next Sunday but that's not why I called. There's an auction at the Spaulding Gallery this afternoon and she said something about wanting to go to it. They have a pretty little walnut canapé, French, that she had her eye on, so I thought I'd pick her up two-ish . . ."

"Wherever she is, she's not expected home until—" He felt as though he had a cloud of stinging gnats around his head. "Oh, five or later."

"Do you think I should bid on the canapé for her?"

"Yes. If she wants it, any price is all right. See you, when? Sunday."

Jane, who had been sitting silently in the corner of the sofa, said, "I'll take the nuisance calls from now on if you want, and just tell everybody she's out and I don't know where."

Titus came back in like the host of the house, with a tray bearing a bottle of scotch and one of Bourbon, three glasses, a bucket of ice, a pitcher of water, and a Coke for Jane.

The phone rang again and with a glance at Devore's white face he answered it.

"Who? Oh, Jane. For you, Jane."

Jane went to the phone and said, "I can't talk, Daddy's expecting an important business call, I'll call you back later."

She heard a rattle of mail in the box outside the front door and went to collect it. She thought her father hadn't heard the little noise, wasn't hearing anything; he was staring in a fixed way at the golds and greens and blues of the Rothko on the wall over the sofa.

Dull mail, bills and junk, a stiff ivory envelope that looked as if it held a wedding announcement, a Bloomingdale's catalogue. And the postcard.

Funny, her mother had a whole pile of this kind of postcard, reproductions of paintings, which she bought at museums and used for quick personal notes to people. Jane always liked to browse through them when she was sick in bed.

Albrecht Dürer's "Violets" on the front. One of her favorites. On the back—

"Daddy," she said. "This is for you."

It was in Rob's handwriting. It held a brief bland message that could send no signal to eavesdropping eyes: "Dad, what you're waiting for is under your brown and white striped shirt at the bottom of the pile in your drawer. R."

Like a teasing affectionate clue to the whereabouts of, say, a birthday present.

Outraged, Jane said, "He used her own postcard for it!"

It was postmarked New York, dated the day before. The cool-headedness of it jarred Devore badly. With the crawl pace of the mail, it must have been posted early in the day, when Madeline was free as air, going about her ordinary morning.

He could hear them agreeing, "It has to be tonight, no matter what. *He'll* be home tomorrow night."

No matter what, no matter how, it has to be tonight.

Titus took the card from his hand. They went, fast, up the stairs together. Jane didn't want to follow them; couldn't. It was all becoming too real, somehow.

There was a folded sheet of white paper in the place indicated. The note was typed and Devore perceived with a cold little flick of anger that his own machine had been used; Rob had sold his Remington to buy film.

"We will want $250,000 to get her back to you. Not new bills in sequence, old bills. Twenties, but throw in one hundred tens and one hundred fives and one hundred singles. Don't bother taking down the serial numbers even if you had time because we know what to do with it. Put the package in the following place: on Route 108A, kind of a back road, there's a brook running east-west about 4 miles north of a town called Ambler, New Jersey, it's on the map. The nearest decent-size town to Ambler is West Portal. 108A runs over the brook on a concrete bridge, with rocks and dry banks under it. Put it behind the big rock on the right as you face west. Your deadline is midnight Thursday. Don't bother to have the police or someone waiting for us there because she won't be released until we're a good distance away, and *not at all* if anything happens to screw things up. It will be seen to that, when we are away, a taxi will be called to pick her up and take her to the bus station, where she can get a bus to New York. And don't bother, either, scratching around Ambler or West Portal, because believe me she's very very far from there." On this communication, there was no initial.

"I wonder," Titus said, remembering Devore quoting Rob early in the summer morning, "if there's a town called Nowhere, New Jersey. Granted that she's anywhere *in* New Jersey, which happens to abut on New York, Pennsylvania, and Delaware. We'll have to try and find her."

"I know," Devore said. "First, the bank."

". . . those four words, 'and not at all' . . ."

"It doesn't take four. It only takes one." He drained his drink. "Pick up the phone, Walter, and call whoever you think you should. But God help us all if the call is wrong."

At the door, he hesitated a moment, his eyes on Jane. It occurred to him that it might not be safe to leave her alone in the house.

"Stay here until I get back?" he asked Titus, who had the receiver off the base and one finger in the dial.

All his walls had fallen down.

9

Madeline thought that Hugh might think it contemptible if she didn't put together and act on some kind of desperate but innately sensible plan.

She summoned his voice.

"Didn't you even try?"

She would have to try.

She was inclined to doubt that Rob would hurt her physically in any final way, but she wasn't at all sure of Mouse Aston. What an inconvenience, what a danger she would be to the girl, a lifetime of danger, with her recording and recollecting eyes and ears.

Mouse might not be able to rest herself thoroughly in the comforting idea that she would keep it all in the family, a private matter, perhaps never forgiven but at least publicly forgotten.

"—Yes, that's the girl." Even under a different name, a different-colored head of hair, even living in Los Angeles or Cannes. She had been freely given Mouse's last name, along with the information that her parents lived in Greenwich.

If that was true; if they didn't live somewhere else, and under another, accurate name. If they were alive at all; but she was somehow sure they were. Something kept Mouse's cold fires of hatred stoked.

No point in getting shot, though, to prove her dauntless courage and independence of spirit.

Her Irish instructress in English, in Rome, who took a kindly motherly interest in her, often said, "You must cut your suit to fit your cloth, Madeline."

Be braced to snatch the opportunity when it came, as it possibly might. They were young and experimenting, after all, on an activity entirely new. Knock the gun from the girl's hand, take her by surprise, slip out of the wine cellar door, bolt *her* in, handle Rob somehow or other, or perhaps he'd be asleep while the girl was on guard duty—

She was about Mouse's height and, she reminded herself, in good physical condition, at least as of yesterday. She had never before used her hands in violence against another human being. But then, she had never before been violently done by. When in Rome . . . Madeline lectured herself. Speaking of Rome.

Rob wasn't entirely sure when, exactly, he began to be afraid of Mouse. Not for himself but for his mother. Perhaps it began when he saw the shining plunge of the needle into the vein inside her arm. And as yet he hadn't defined or even admitted the fear to himself.

"You and your rats," he said when Mr. Cove and the McIntoshes had taken their leave. "Great idea, but—"

"You have to play this kind of thing by ear," Mouse said, as though crime was her regular pursuit. She added complacently, "I got the idea from my own name, actually."

"Well, the next thing you know he'll have an exterminator out here. Everybody hates rats. And the big season for unloading houses, summer places, is on, he'll want to take care of it in a hurry."

He was fixing his mother's lunch. Thinly sliced cucumber on lightly buttered whole-wheat bread, a quartered tomato; he reached for salt and pepper. Maybe a cup of hot soup, it wasn't all that warm in the cellar. He opened a can of beef consommé and poured it into a little pot.

When she had guests to lunch, she usually served them white wine. He uncorked a bottle of inexpensive Chablis he had brought along for this purpose.

Not wanting her to leap ahead of him again, he said, "We'll have to move her out of the cellar, right after lunch, into that tower room or whatever it is."

"You'd make a great waiter, or cook, for somebody," Mouse said. "Yes, of course we'll have to move her. There's a screwdriver in the tool drawer on the right. You'll have to find a nice bolt and put it on the door of that room."

Stung by her reference to his lunch preparations, he said, "This kitchen is one hell of a mess, when are you going to clean it up? We don't want people, if there are any more people, noticing things, complaining about things—"

"Me? Clean it up? What year are you in, Robbie?" She laughed softly. "The word, like in everything else we're doing, is 'we.'"

The soup had started boiling. He took it off the burner.

"What if she, Ma, screamed or something when she hears somebody else if they turn up here going through the house . . . ?"

"I've been working on that."

She got up and went to the wall phone. A telephone directory hung on a nail beside it. She leafed through it, found a number, and dialed.

Jesus, what was she up to now?

"Let me speak to Mr. Cove, please," she said, and then, "He's still out? No, no message, I'll call him back."

"What—?"

"I'll practice on you, you're Mr. Cove. Mr. Cove, I didn't want to discuss my business in front of strangers but my friend is interested in this house, his parents sent him down with me to look it over, it's pretty well like the kind of place they said they wanted. But we need like time to get the feel of it, can you hold off any other prospects until, say—today's Wednesday—until Friday?" She produced a convincing giggle. "And we're not only house-hunting, Mr. Cove, we're having like, you know, a private party here."

She ran her tongue over her upper lip. "That'll scare him off, he'll be afraid of opening the front door and finding us running around naked. And this place has been on the market for months, how can he be sure we're not going to take it off his hands?"

"That sounds all right," Rob said, strangely put off by her racing ingenuity. "That sounds good, Mouse."

He was arranging plate, wineglass, handled Sèvres soup cup, napkin and silver on the tray.

You'd make a great waiter.

He said sulkily, "If you don't mind, I'd prefer to go alone. This time."

"You're kidding. She could snatch the tray and heave it all, hot soup, silver, broken glass, right in your face. Where again's the gun?"

He got it from the top of the white cabinet and thrust it in the back pocket of his coverall.

Then he picked up the tray, both hands engaged, and Mouse came over and took the gun out of his pocket.

"You don't know about these things, you might shoot yourself in the ass," she explained kindly. "And about seeing your mother alone, no, never. She might try to get at you. Oh my dear beloved son, my firstborn. Or cry. From when I used to have my nose in a book—Hamlet and all that—conscience makes cowards of us, or something."

She opened the cellar door and he followed her. As they went down the stairs, she said, "By the way, you haven't been to bed. You'd better go right after this."

"Maybe later. I'm not sleepy."

"You're not going to be any good to me if you conk out on your feet," she prodded.

To *me*. Hand on the helm again.

It wasn't her mother and it wasn't her father's money.

They had made a very clear arrangement about the money: share and share alike if they stayed together, fifty thousand for Mouse if they split up and if there was any of it left by then.

Not now, not yet, not with the two of them, Madeline instructed herself as they came into the wine cellar.

She had been standing for half an hour close to the door, with the heavy red-bound volume of Shakespeare in her hand. The weight of it made her arm ache. Quickly and accurately thrown, it might have dealt with Mouse's gun. If Mouse had been alone.

Hearing the bolt, she just had time to place the book innocently on the card table.

Rob set the tray down on the table. "Brushing up on your Shakespeare, Ma?" He tried to make it easy, casual, but his voice was raw.

"Heavy reading, literally, I mean," Mouse said, eyes on the book. "Somehow or other I think—" She picked it up. Goodbye to this possible weapon.

"I found it a bit hard to concentrate on Richard the Third," Madeline said in her soft clear voice, "because I was wondering what your arrangements were, your timetable."

She gazed thoughtfully at the glass of Chablis and the cucumber sandwich.

"Dad kind of loused up the timetable, getting home a day early," Rob said. "We were going to give him the best part of a day to get . . . things together. Just as well, he'll have a little more time. If everything's all right, you'll be heading back home Friday morning."

"Today, I think, is Wednesday?"

"For God's *sake*, Ma, of course it's Wednesday." The question, the vagueness in her voice, worried him; had something happened to her head?

"We might as well stay here until she's had her lunch, and then move her," Mouse said.

It took all Madeline's strength of will not to pick up her wineglass and hurl it into the girl's face. Not a woman, not anybody, just merchandise to be arranged, shelved.

She reached for her sandwich. I must, I must. "Do you have someone else you want to accommodate in the cellar, is that why I'm to be moved?" she asked.

Her question went unanswered; they exchanged warning glances.

Then Rob mumbled, "It's a bit chilly down here, damp—"

"Hey, you'd better fix the—uh—hardware, Rob. Before we all go up."

Another prison to be prepared.

Chew, swallow, sip; you must. It was a long time, until Friday morning, if there was ever to be such a thing as a Friday morning waiting for her.

10

Mouse was packing everything on the step stool into the suit-case. She efficiently stripped the mattress of its sheets and blanket, deflated and folded it, and made a neat pile with the pillow on top. Madeline saw her eyes flicking the stone room, checking; readying it for someone else's inquiring gaze? Whose?

She managed all but the tomato. Rob came back, breathing hard as though he'd been doing something at a run.

"All set?" Mouse asked. "Robbie, you take this junk, along with the tray—" and they went in an orderly fashion, single file, Rob in front of her, Mouse in back, an odd family party, up the stairs into the kitchen. Madeline was surprised to see day, hour, reestablish itself. Bright sun outside, heavy deep green shadow, a June sparkling, the sound of a bird, a thrush, she thought. Twelve-thirty give or take a few minutes on a smiling summer noon.

The bedroom in the cupola, two flights up from the ground floor, was small, octagon-shaped and many-windowed, but the windows were all stained glass except one narrow one, over-looking the drive, which must have at some time been broken. The purple and olive glass had been replaced with a clear sheet.

Mouse, making the bed, said to Rob, "Reminds you of church, doesn't it?"

The bed was narrow, a close relative of a cot. There was a small slipper chair, a white wooden stand with a sink in it, and an oval rag rug. Madeline thought its gloom of stormy color must once have imprisoned some hapless servant.

Rob stood at the window, looking out, while Mouse completed her bedmaking. She had handed him the gun to hold and her eyes remained on his hand, and on it, while she tucked sheets and folded blankets, her body braced like a bow.

Madeline wondered about the menial chore performed for an adult by this girl; and concluded that it was meant to make her feel very much under the contemptuous control of her warders.

The room was stuffy and smelled of moth repellent and elapsed time, and a memory of damp wood. It had been a wet spring. Rob laid the gun on the windowsill and put his hands to the heavy latch that worked the casement window.

In a portion of a moment, Madeline gently leaned forward, for the gun, and in doing so saw the sun glinting on the windshield of some vehicle at a far curve of the drive, coming toward the house.

And then she was struck by a pillow hurled from four feet away. She stumbled back and half fell into the slipper chair.

"Goddam fool," Mouse said. Not to her.

"Ma needs air." He had not yet reduced her to "she" or "her."

"I would like," Madeline said carefully, "to go to the bathroom before I'm locked in."

Rob had the window open now. June air fanned her cheeks. She made no mention of the flash on the windshield, and deliberately assumed a crestfallen air because the try for the gun had failed.

There was a mean narrow bathroom with a frosted glass window at a half-landing below the cupola room. "Do not," a

Victorian voice intoned, "spoil the help." An old, small tub with a tongue of rust underneath a dripping faucet, a similarly stained sink with no shield over its discolored metal underpipes, a curling linoleum floor patterned in a bronze and green imitation of Wilton carpeting. Spider webs in all the ceiling corners and a very large active spider wandering about in the sink.

Mouse sat down on the edge of the tub.

"Would you mind leaving me alone—except for the spider?"

"You make the rules in your house," Mouse said. "We make the rules here."

"You do, you mean."

Madeline took her little striped case out of her pocket and started to brush her teeth.

This morning, Mouse had left her alone, waited outside the door. She too must have noticed the approach of whatever it was, up the drive, and perhaps was afraid her charge would start screaming.

With a very great effort, she took off her trouser suit and her pants and bra, in front of this darkly watching girl.

"*Another* shower?" Mouse asked impatiently.

The shower curtain had once been white but was now grayed and mildewed. An antique arrangement was looped over the hot and cold water handles, a ring to hang around your neck, with little holes to drip water over you, and a rotting rubber hose. There was a towel rack against the wall over the tub. On it was an unstylish harsh white terry towel, long and wide.

Mouse removed herself to the toilet seat. Madeline got into the tub, turned on the water, let it run from its ring over her, and shielded by the shower curtain took the towel and made a large heavy knot in one end of it.

She put the knotted towel on the bottom of the tub and left it there getting soaked, to add weight. Under Mouse's cynically examining eyes, she stepped out, pulled the curtain back across its bar, and reached for a towel from the other rack, on the opposite wall.

She put her clothes back on and took a comb from the plastic case. "Would you mind moving so I can see in the medicine-cabinet mirror?"

Mouse got up and in a swift whirl Madeline reached for the towel in the tub and swung it hard. The knot struck Mouse at the side of her head. She fell, crashing backward, into the little stained tub.

"Rob," she screamed, *"Rob!"*

Rob was tired of his mechanic's coverall. Well, he'd practically lived in it since early yesterday. Tuesday? He was getting as bad as she was about what day it was. The coverall had by now unpleasant associations, the blanket-wrapped body held to it, the sweating night drive, the gun recently snatched imperiously from the pocket of it. He wasn't old enough to know that garments you wore while doing something you basically disapproved of had a secret soil of their own.

He remembered from previous exploration that Grace Aston's brother kept some old but good clothes in the big bedroom to the left of the landing. While Mouse attended his mother in the bathroom, he chose a pair of gray flannel trousers and a black and white striped shirt. He went down to the kitchen for the red-handled scissors he had spotted, came back up again and cut the trousers into shorts.

He looked at the scissors in his hand, and went into the bathroom that opened off the bedroom. Rapidly, without thinking much about it, he cut a lot of his hair off, into careless jagged locks. He flushed the golden shining discarded hair down the toilet. He looked without knowing it several years younger and considerably more male.

He wasn't consciously thinking about his hair or his clothing. He had a mental picture of opening the front door, sometime when Mouse was asleep, and saying, Run, Ma, *run . . .*

Crazy, it was just that he needed sleep, or would soon.

Anyway, Mouse might wake up in the middle of it, and there was no way of being sure what she would do, with that gun. To either of them.

It was a funny way to put it, but it was safer for his mother to stay neatly kidnapped, to be ransomed, than to change or break or interrupt the pattern. She would be safer, that is, from Mouse, if they all went along and played it straight.

He was tying the striped shirttails into a butterfly knot over his rib cage when he heard Mouse's scream. For a second he thought it was his mother's and he stood still in panic. Then his legs made themselves move.

The brown van was parked in the drive at the front of the house, at the foot of the wooden porch steps.

The sign painted on its doors had once said "Parker and Parelli, Exterminators." But customers objected, they didn't want the word describing their private problems proclaimed from their driveways for all the world to see, so a black bar had been painted over the company's function.

Jimmy Parker, Jr., had had a late night and was not only drowsy but hungry. The rats could wait. He took his brown paper bag and went and sat down under a big maple tree. His mother had provided two liverwurst sandwiches on rye bread, with plenty of sliced onion, a can of beer still dewed with cold, a chocolate-iced doughnut, and an apple.

He finished his food and his beer and closed his eyes, breathed over by soft air and the smell of grass and clover. He drifted delightfully off.

Madeline ran down the half flight of stairs to the first landing and then the long flight to the hall. She heard from some step above, "Get the car—that van—unless I get her first—" Mouse.

Rob, "But *he's* out there under the tree—"

The bolt on the front door—

She didn't know whether Hugh was telling her now, or from years back, or both.

"Lift it a little before you begin to slide it back, Madeline."

She obeyed, and the door seemed to fling itself open. Cross the porch, tear open the screen door—in her haste and fear she almost fell down the steep porch stairs.

She fumbled with the door handle of the brown van, with a strong instinctive feeling that from some near window a gun was trained on her, accurately.

She had caught when she went down the steps a lightning image of the sleeping gangly boy under the maple tree. It wouldn't be a good idea for them to wake him up by shooting her. There would be the body to explain, halfway into his van.

She slid behind the wheel. The working of the stick shift puzzled her for a moment. Then her hand remembered. Hugh had long ago had a brief love affair with a vintage Jaguar XK 120. She turned the key in the ignition and started the van and hadn't gone twenty yards before she saw in the mirror the gray car close behind her, Rob driving it.

The curves of the driveway were unsafe for speeding, and her handling of any vehicle was at best cautious and conservative. But her foot on the accelerator was doing the thinking for her now, taking her fast past the rhododendrons.

The gray car went faster, drew level with her, a terrifying few inches from the van, surely they'd crash—

I tried, Hugh, I did try—

But suicide isn't the answer to anything. She was forced bumpingly into deep grass beside the gravel. With a showy scream of tires, Rob's car flung itself ahead of her and sideways across the drive. She braked violently, bruising herself against the wheel, and came to a stop nine or ten inches away from him.

Rob got out and came over to her. She saw that he was trembling and wondered vacantly what had happened to his hair.

He opened the door of the van and said, "Move over, Ma. Don't make me do anything to you. Please."

She moved over. She found nothing to say. In silence, they went back.

Jimmy Parker was standing at the porch steps, helplessly shouting and waving his fists. Rob drove rapidly past him to the rear of the house, where Mouse was waiting on the step outside the open kitchen door. He leaned across Madeline to open the van door and she was pulled out with force and speed. The gun was dragging down the breast pocket of Mouse's shirt.

"*Help!*" she cried, before Mouse's strong palm was clasped across her mouth. The kitchen door closed on the two of them and Mouse reached for her pocket.

Rob drove the van to the front. The less said, he thought, the better.

Getting out, he told Jimmy Parker, "She's a bit mental. Can't resist other people's cars. We can't break her of the habit."

Jimmy Parker, confused but relieved, said agreeingly, "This town is full of nuts. Yesterday I did for a woman who has twenty-nine cats. You ought to smell the place. Cockroaches, was her trouble. Naturally not mice. Well, I'll get at your rats now."

Reporting his day's work to his father later, he said, "I thought I heard her shout for help but the kid said she was mental. She looked it, the little I saw of her through the window, she looked sort of like a ghost herself, isn't that place supposed to be haunted? Anyway, there wasn't a sign of rats, somebody's crazy, but a job's a job and I sprayed the cellars good, spent an hour down there. Before I left I stuffed a sack with old newspaper, like, bodies, you know, in case they were looking out the window."

His father beamed approvingly. "Good boy. Have a beer. Here's to Aston's rats."

11

At the exact moment when the car Rob was driving screamed and slewed and blocked the van his mother was driving, Devore felt a terrible clutch under his ribs.

"Hugh . . . *oh, please* . . ."

Indigestion, probably, or hunger, he had had no lunch.

Or maybe not. As with people long and deeply in love they lived in a way in each other's minds, sometimes started to say the same thing at the same time, from one corner of the sofa to the other or from Paris, or San Francisco, to New York.

Malcolm Copeland, president of the Copeland Banking and Trust Company, saw the spring of sweat on the broad forehead, the grimace as though a spasm of pain had struck.

"Awkward kind of thing, your own boy," he mused, to fill the silence that had fallen over their tight low-voiced conversation. "But, first things first."

They had gone to school together and were casual on-and-off friends. Access to Copeland money had helped Devore in his early days.

He forced himself back to the moment, this matter of attending to immediate business, and looked across the tidy desk. Copeland, in his thin fine heather tweeds and with his fresh crisply featured pink face looked like a Scottish laird, not a New York banker. His own only son had died when his motorcycle hit a tree in Wilton, Connecticut.

"Sometimes," he said, "you wonder, Hugh."

There was a delicate knock at the door and his attractive young secretary came in with a tray.

"You don't mind if I have a bite? Anything for you?"

"No, nothing, thanks."

Copeland's bite was a sandwich of caviar and chopped hard-boiled egg on thin black bread, and a glass of champagne to go with it. Devore had observed him eating this collation on other and less desperate occasions. Copeland explained, "If you're rich you might as well enjoy it. And not many calories, you know."

There wasn't, Copeland assured him, going to be any problem about the money. Not with the building.

The building was Devore House on East Fifty-eighth Street. New Yorkers and visitors enjoyed it. It was strong and graceful, both a rest and an excitement to the eye, twelve stories high, faced with cool gray-green marble, built around a center square. The square could be entered freely, by anyone. From the west rooftop, a wall-wide waterfall rushed and silvered into an oblong pool below, a delightful midtown music. There were lusty white birches around the pool. The wall opposing the waterfall was an unbroken sheet of plate-glass mirror, which echoed light and water and rainbows into the offices facing the square as though they were on a ship at sea. Devore Associates occupied the top two floors.

"He kindly tells you not to bother with the serial numbers but we'll scan them anyway, in case you want them later," Copeland said. He wondered what he would do in Devore's situation. Take it like the knockdown blow it was and sag down, stretch out, under it; and place the secret in the family vault? Or fight back, hunt him down, the family criminal? "Unfortunately," he went on, "Washington has given the uninitiated lessons on how to cleanse marked money. Well. You probably have a lot of things to see to. We'll get right on it."

They discussed details briefly. Copeland would have a messenger deliver the money at a time to be agreed upon, on

Thursday afternoon. It would be placed in the trunk of Devore's Mercedes. Devore took the trunk and garage keys off his key ring and handed them over. Yes, he said, the garage was securely lockable (" . . . as securely as anything is these days, if they can't do anything with the lock they'll take the doors off, but this doesn't seem to be the time to worry about it"). Yes, only one other person had a key to the garage, his friend and tenant Walter Titus. And of course Rob had his key, but at the moment Rob didn't count.

"You surely can get a policeman to keep an eye on the garage tomorrow," Copeland said. "If the police are going to enter into this thing at all, that is." His voice indicated that it was none of his business.

Devore got up from his chair. "Thank you for all this, Malcolm," he said. "I suppose the police are right now waiting for me."

Cold accountant's eyes on him. Inspector Joseph Blaney, from Police Headquarters on Centre Street. Titus's connections being what they were, and Devore being who he was, and the matter in hand being what it was. Too big for the precinct house.

The eyes said at first, You fixed this up, get a quarter of a million in cash out of some lame-legged business. You and your wife and your son.

And called us in to make it look okay if insurance people or your partners or somebody started sniffing around.

Not a bad idea, if you could get away with it. "And you say that the note was—mmm—typed on your own machine? Because he'd hocked or sold his or whatever?"

Devore got the message accurately and took a firm hold on his fury. They lived with crooks. Deception, violence, vileness was their daily bread. No one ever called in the police to say, Look how nice, how quiet, how well-conducted and on the level everything here is.

There were five of them in the living room. Devore, Blaney,

Titus, and two men in their middle thirties from the FBI, both in gray suits, both lean and unremarkable-looking, both now waiting, listening, while Blaney got in his licks, the local man rating the first turn.

Devore hadn't wanted Jane present. He sent her over to the Bolands'. When he came in she had whispered to him, tears in her eyes, "I thought and thought, I thought myself into a horrible headache, Daddy, but I still can't remember where—"

He bent and put an arm around her shoulder. "Maybe if you wouldn't try so hard."

"And anyway, they might have just been talking about somewhere they were going to go and spend the night," Jane said forthrightly. "She could have roommates in the way and . . ."

"Possibly," Devore said. Exhortation and pressure could force it deeper into the recesses of Jane's mind, sink it without a trace. And having, unknowingly, relied so much on a flash of recollection, he was now bitterly inclined to dismiss the whole idea.

Jane, innocently deep in the antique horrors of *Dracula*, hearing disconnected syllables, associating them with blood and werewolves. Barely listening, bored with lovers, but thinking she could have heard something that might be helpful—

Perhaps really wanting center stage, attention, a way of re-establishing herself now that her mother was gone and Rob had turned out not to be Rob but a frightening stranger.

"Have you had your lunch?"

"Yes, a peanut-butter sandwich. I made you ham and cheese and put it in the refrigerator, will you be sure and eat it?" His pallor and the tired dark gray blaze of his eyes behind his glasses distressed her. The roof of her world was shaking in a battering wind.

"I promise, and thanks, Jane. You run off now." He added lightly, "The Bolands probably have an atlas around somewhere, you might take a look at New Jersey. Oh, and all the states around it—"

Before going out the front door, she turned. "I've left a list of all the people I thought he knew, and telephone numbers and addresses when I could pin them down. *He* never tells me anything, but it's just sort of what I come on, or when I hear them—and he might have said something to someone. Like 'Guess what *I'm* going to do.'"

She seemed not to want to speak her brother's name.

"Good, very helpful," Devore said. "You may be wanted later, I'll let you know."

He had no immediate appetite for his sandwich but he wanted a drink. While he was in the kitchen getting it, one of the FBI men said to Blaney, "I don't think there's any malarkey about this. He's solid as a rock. We checked him. Contracts for a university library in Colorado. And a mixed-use building in Dallas, forty stories. And something or other in India."

The three men in their different efficient ways put their claws and their beaks into vulnerable parts of Devore; who looked, however, powerfully self-sustaining even in his private disaster.

Titus sat silent and listening in a wing chair and wondered if he had made an awful mistake, summoning the experts.

Experts?

Men.

The FBI agents had properly unmemorable names to go with their clothes and faces. One was Brown and one was Lister.

It was Lister who asked, "What do you think brought about this crisis? Revenge? Was he in trouble with you, was he being punished for something?"

"Par for the course now, I suppose, he dropped out of college and was told he'd have to find work, something to do, no more money from home forthcoming."

"I suppose that would be enough," Brown said doubtfully.

Devore looked not at him but at Blaney's hard expressionless face. "Before we go any further, I in my day have taken strong—and wrong—positions and retreated from them when the light dawned. My son may very well do the same thing. I assume that if he changes his mind about going through with this you'll drop it?"

"Well, now, Mr. Devore, you've set something in motion." Blaney lit a cigarette, taking his time. Spoiled rich kid, he thought, you asked for it, Mr. Devore. If it really was his son's idea, if it was a straight kidnapping. In all his years of dirty work, he'd never come on anything like this.

The house impressed him and against his will Devore impressed him and he resented that.

"From where we sit, if it stops being a kidnapping it stops being a crime," Brown said mildly.

Blaney turned on him. "If the bank robber decided he didn't want the money after all and dropped it on the front steps on the way out, would you let him go? Let's get on with it. Unless time is no importance whatever to you, Mr. Devore."

The look he got back was as hard as his own.

They got on with it. The postcard, the ransom directions. Have you a picture of your son? Yes. Picture produced from a scramble in the library desk drawer: Rob at eighteen, playing tennis in Greens Farms, taken by Jane with her Instamatic.

And who do you think "we" is? Are?

He said he had no idea but he thought it might be a girl. He hesitated before going on. Was this fair? Perhaps an unknown innocent jeaned girl guzzling Coke somewhere, pulled in by the police and questioned about her participation in crime, in outrage . . . Just because Jane had found a kind of darkness in her, and because that kid on the telephone, hunting her, sounded—what?—tough, evasive, but seeming to take for granted that where Rob was, Mouse was.

Titus cleared his throat. Devore glanced at him. "The last girl he was seen with was named, nicknamed, Mouse, I don't know her last name." He gave them Jane's description, leaving out the nuances. And added uncomfortably, "It may not be—I mean he has the usual collection of girls you'd expect at his age."

He felt in his pocket. "Here's a list of his friends, both sexes, my daughter made it, I'm away from home a good deal."

Hangouts, they asked him, bars where he met people and talked to them?

"I don't think he goes to bars—they don't. The only place I know of is a coffeehouse called the Clipjoint on Bleecker Street."

"What's he on, Mr. Devore?" Blaney asked, and Devore, who disapproved of the severity of the New York State laws concerning the individual possession and use of marijuana, said, "Nothing."

"For a dangerous kid," Blaney said with a faint and mirthless laugh, "he's got nice clean habits. No drinking, no pot."

There wasn't the faintest flicker in Devore's gray gaze. "An occasional beer."

Picture of Madeline (one he carried in his billfold to refresh himself when he was far away from her, sitting on the grass under a tree on the lawn of the house in Greens Farms, caught in a dapple of spring sunlight and half smiling at his camera). Description of Madeline, age, height, coloring, any special identifying marks, and had he any idea what she had been wearing? Possibly a nightgown, the bed had been slept in, or at least occupied, and there was a pink summer blanket missing.

Did his son have a car? Yes, it was in the garage.

Could his neighbor have been mistaken about the Greens Farms house being empty? Were there cellars?

"I called the police up there while we were waiting for you and had them check," the quiet Titus said from his wing chair. "The house is empty cellar to attic."

Were there any other places the family went, vacation cottages, things like that, places he'd know how to get into? No.

Had Robert Devore ever been arrested for anything? "No, not that I know of."

Blaney eyed the FBI men. "You'll check anyway—you people are very big on records and fingerprints. If he'd been picked up for something while he was away at school they'd know in Jersey."

What places did he visit when he was away from home? Reasonably near, that is.

Lenox, Massachusetts. Nantucket. Westport, Connecticut. Princeton and environs, of course. Charleston, South Carolina. St. Albans, Vermont. And he had gone to summer camp between the ages of ten and twelve at Newburgh, New York.

His heart sank as he considered the map of New York and New England and points south.

Which of the thousands and thousands of towns was named Nowhere?

12

"How did you—uh—get along with your wife, Mr. Devore?" Blaney asked casually.

Devore stared at him; at the stained sharp eyes. The dark blood came up under his skin.

"You mean, did she have herself kidnapped in some kind of revenge on me? She and Rob to split the money?" His voice wasn't raised but it rang through the high airy room.

"We have to look at all the angles," Blaney said. "This isn't a parlor game, you know."

"As a very old friend," Titus said, "I can vouch for the fact that they are a most affectionate couple."

Of course they would get to Jane, and they did now. At the neighbors'? Would he mind calling her and asking her to come home? A few words—

"I'm going to be grilled," a tense and waiting Jane said to Elizabeth Boland. "By the police." And then in a rush of shame and rage at herself, "Mr. Titus has been robbed, I think, a burglar, and they may have an idea I saw something from my bedroom window, which I didn't."

Going straight to her father, she murmured anxiously, "Their puppy—Lucinda, she's a St. Bernard, ten weeks old—chewed up part of their Hammond's atlas, and they threw it away. We looked and looked but we couldn't find any maps. I didn't want to ask Mrs. Boland because she'd want to know why."

Into her ear, he murmured back, "That's all right, skip it for the moment."

To hand her over to these men, strangers, formidable, pounding away at her memory, might put out the tiny flicker there completely. However unpromising, irrelevant it might turn out to be, left to itself to surface.

Sitting beside him on the sofa, she felt calm and safe and answered their questions clearly and directly.

Had Rob had any kind of disagreement, fight, with his mother while his father was away?

No. "My mother doesn't have quarrels with people."

Did she know of any trouble her brother was in, something he'd need a lot of money to get out of, something he hadn't told his parents about?

No.

Did he have any friends—boys or girls—with jail records, or who had been in bad trouble at home or with the police?

"Rob's very choosy. There's nobody I know of like that."

Well, now. Girls.

"I gave Daddy the list—the ones I know of—but Angie's gone to Turkey and Barbara Briggs got a concussion water skiing. I think he broke off with that girl he was living with last winter but she's there anyway."

"You met his last girl. Mouse?" Blaney grimaced at the name.

"I . . . saw her. I heard her. I didn't *meet* her."

"Would you say she's your brother's best girl right now? I mean, does he like her?"

Jane considered, and said, "'Like' isn't the right word, he's crazy about her." A rage which she didn't understand, against Mouse, was welling up in her and before she could stop herself she added, "I think she'd do *anything*—and make *him* do anything—"

Two voices, talking at once.

Blaney, harsh: "Look here, young woman, confederates or no confederates, your brother's number one in this picture, don't try to—"

Lister, or Brown: "If someone's to release her when they're off and running there must be at least a third pair of hands . . ."

A long finger of sunlight buried itself in the shimmer of Jane's hair. Smoke fumed blue around Blaney's head. Lister was taken by a fit of sneezing. Devore blinked, and was overcome by a sudden sense of unreality and looked at his watch to reassure himself that it was a definite time of day on a real day in a real world. Two minutes after two o'clock.

And she had to stay alive, she must, until at least twelve o'clock tomorrow night, by which time she would have been paid for.

Hang on, Madeline. Darling. Look obedient, and subdued. Don't do anything to make them nervous.

Don't light any fuse attached to your own body.

He must have missed a couple of sentences; the three men got up to go. Lister, who had a kind heart under his gray suit, said to Devore, "I want to restate what we stated when we came in—the first object is to get Mrs. Devore home safe and sound. There won't be any boats rocked in that direction, believe me, Mr. Devore."

"I'd like to," Devore said, looking at Inspector Blaney, "and thanks."

Within an hour, jeaned young men with hairstyles to match were asking casual questions here and there, or drinking espresso with a twist of lemon.

"Hey, I just got in from Denver, I'm hunting Rob, have you seen him?"

"Rob—Rob Devore—borrowed a camera off me and I want it back. He's not home, do you know where I can find him?"

"Mouse swore she'd meet me here, do you know where she

is?" "*Mouse*. Mouse who?" "I thought everyone knew Mouse, you're just not with it, man."

"Rob's girl what's-her-name is sore as hell. Who's this new one? I heard she's bad news."

At the Clipjoint, Halligan continued drinking espresso; he would much have preferred beer. He signaled a long-haired waitress in huge dark glasses. Almost black in here, and with those glasses, how did she see to serve?

"Mouse been in? Today or yesterday?"

"Not today. And I was off yesterday."

She must know Mouse then, she showed no surprise at the name.

"I forget where she lives—do you know?"

"Haven't a clue, sorry."

He fumbled in his pocket. "I have this birthday card for her and, crazy, I don't even know how to spell her last name. Maybe you could help me?" He had appealing blue eyes and freckles.

Al Madonna was sitting at a table one foot away from him.

The waitress said, "I wish I could, but she's kind of new to me, I don't know her last name. I know Rob Devore, of course, she goes with him. Why don't you call up Rob Devore?"

Al smelled the law, no matter what clothes it had on or how its hair was cut.

He had gone up to Yonkers to see to the state of Daybreak's health and spirits—both highly satisfactory—and to take care of his indignant trainer's back pay. Then he resumed his pursuit of Mouse.

He thoughtfully sipped his café Valencia—orange slice and grenadine—not showing a sign of his intense interest. He'd been right. Mouse was into something, up to something. Or maybe on to something. It had to be something fairly big or fairly good or the police wouldn't be looking for her.

This poor slob would probably have to sit here all afternoon and half the night trying to find out about her, her last name, and where she hung out.

But *he* wasn't stuck at the Clipjoint, he was free as air, to look for her.

Out of town, maybe? With Rob Devore. Where? Anywhere. Where would someone up to something lie low? You'd want, he thought, a place you knew, but that everyone else didn't necessarily know about. A place where you were in, sort of, control.

He suddenly remembered a fantastic weekend with her early in May at her aunt's empty house in—what was that town in Jersey?

He went to a pay phone and called Evelyn something again. "Sorry to bother you, but I just had an idea—would you know if Mouse went off with a suitcase, an overnight case? That way I could forget it for the moment if I knew for sure she's out of town."

"Wait, I'll look in her closet." And then, "Yes, her yellow beach bag or whatever it is is missing, she uses that when she goes away for a day or two. If you're all that interested, do you want to leave your name? And then she can get in touch with you when she gets back."

"Thanks," Al said. "Mike Finch."

Now he remembered the name of the town. Prudence. Nothing kind of town but loaded with money, off the map so to speak, the end of nowhere.

It was a nice day and he had nothing better to do, it wouldn't hurt to take a run to Jersey on a long shot.

He went to a garage near his apartment on Carmine Street and got out the white Chevrolet convertible that was only partly paid for. It would be nice to have a real job, a second-hand Ferrari, a Jag, but people noticed and recalled special makes and colors of cars and he wanted his to be useful but anonymous, whatever his business in it happened to be.

To get the taste of the café Valencia out of his mouth, he went into a bar and had two scotches on the rocks and a

Swiss-cheese sandwich on rye. Then he got into the car and to refresh his memory checked the map of New Jersey which he found shuffled among its fellows under the front seat.

It took him a minute or so to find it. Then his fingernail landed on it. Prudence, here I come.

13

Mouse kept her hand over Madeline's mouth and the gun at the small of her back.

"Move," she said. "Quick. Back up there."

Her prisoner for a moment had been motionless. No struggling after her capture, and not a word out of her. Mouse sensed a letting go of muscles, a body in defeat.

"If you yell again, or make any noise at all, I'll use this—"

"Yes, probably." The voice had lost its soft clarity and sounded small and very tired.

Fast motion wasn't possible with Mouse clamped to her.

"Walk ahead of me again. And remember."

She saw the almond eyes, with a faint bluish color under them that wasn't makeup, flick to the kitchen wall phone.

"I wouldn't try it if I were you," she said. "And there's only one other one, and it doesn't happen to be on your route."

They were halfway up the second flight of stairs when Rob's voice, deliberately loud, could be heard from the kitchen.

"The cellar door's here—I hope, by the way, you took out the ignition key, she might try it again, she gets out of her room—"

On the step below her as they climbed, Mouse said, "He's told him, you heard him, that you're out of your head, so even if you did make a noise while he's in the house— But I think you'd be smarter not to."

Madeline, wordless, went into the cupola room and walked over to the bed and lay down on it, her face to the wall.

Rob came in and looked at her. He said to Mouse, "You didn't hurt her, did you?"

Mouse merely raised her eyebrows and Rob bent close and saw the red marks Mouse's hand had left about his mother's mouth and cheeks. Her eyes were closed.

An enormous inertia had descended on her. Aftershock, she supposed. Tags of their voices seemed to come from far away.

". . . do you think he'll be long, down there?"

". . . how do I know, he probably charges by the hour, he might be there till tomorrow night . . ."

"You're a big help. Go to bed. You're ahead of time with your new hairdo but . . ."

". . . not sleepy, yet . . ."

". . . crazy, but I have this feeling you don't trust me . . ."

". . . crazy is right . . ."

Madeline took the basic retreat. In a way insultingly, to both of her powerful young captors, she went deeply to sleep.

Reaching Prudence, Al Madonna reminded himself that when there was big money around, there were police around to keep their eye on it. He observed the speed limits scrupulously. Twenty miles per hour, the sign just before the village green said. Then a sign beyond it allowed him thirty miles per hour.

He went past a red-tile-roofed white palace, on a hillside, that he thought would be nice to live in. Not, to him, an impossible dream, but something that could happen one of these days, the way things had been going, Detroit and Daybreak and all.

He turned left between the obelisk-shaped granite gateposts and up the long curved drive. He saw the brown Parker and Parelli van parked at the front steps and was puzzled; it didn't look like Mouse's style, a van.

He parked his car at the side of the house, next to the

neglected herbaceous border where the Oriental poppies and the blue bearded iris grew, got out and went back to the van and looked into it. A green tin can on the floor said "Rat-Erase."

He correctly surmised an exterminator on the premises. You didn't, he said to himself, have those kind of people around if you were only staying for a day, or a weekend.

The jealousy he had been holding back, because he didn't like to waste emotion, energy, until needed and summoned, clasped him hotly.

He climbed the wooden steps, opened the porch door, and allowed his rage to cause a sudden thunder on the brass knocker in the shape of a lion's head.

The call to Mr. Cove had been made. ("He didn't quite believe me but he didn't *not* believe me either. He said okay, nobody until Friday afternoon, and asked if we knew the price and I said we did, no problem.")

No chance visitors were expected at Grace Aston's house.

It was an island of summer silence, green and remote, with only their two voices, and the sleeping woman upstairs, the bolt on her door driven home. And Jimmy Parker, doing whatever exterminators do, in the cellars.

At the appalling noise from the hall, Rob said in a whisper, "Jesus Christ."

Mouse went into the living room and put her eye to a hairline parting in the dark red curtains on the side window looking onto the porch.

She heard the light noise in her own throat; a gasp.

He would have seen the van, of course. If he went on crashing away at the knocker, the boy downstairs would sooner or later hear him and come blundering up. She didn't think he would take no, to the knocker, for an answer.

She murmured over her shoulder to Rob, standing struck with purple and scarlet light, "Al. Let's mind our manners. We're here for a picnic, that's all."

She opened the door, and Al said, "Hi, Mouse," and walked confidently in.

He was wearing tight white jeans, a white silk shirt from Sulka patterned in gold fleurs-de-lis, and white espadrilles. His eyes sparkled with avid curiosity in his brown blunt pitted face. They went to Mouse's face between the long sweeps of her dark hair, to Rob's.

"I swore I'd find you and what d'you know I did find you," he said. He kept in his pocket for the moment the fact that the police were looking for her too. "And what are you doing in this particular neck of the woods, Mousie?"

Rob's savagely barbered hair had already arranged itself into thick petals. He brushed it out of his eyebrows with the back of his hand. His forehead was wet.

"A day or so in the country," he said. "We're getting our health back. Fresh air, long walks, plenty of sleep, *you* know."

Al went a dark furious red but held on to his composure.

"Sure, I know," he said. He walked past them into the living room and went and sat down solidly on the sofa.

"I call this the Al and Mouse Memorial Couch," he said. "Remember, Mouse? Wild."

"I don't like to be rude but this is a private party," Mouse said. She had dropped her street voice and now spoke pure Miss Porter's. "As long as you dropped in, though, a drink? I'm afraid we have only beer, or perhaps a glass of Chablis?"

She didn't have to remind Rob this time. He went to the kitchen and took the gun off the counter and put it back on top of the cabinet. Her voice called after him, "He'll take a glass of wine, he says, if it's well chilled," and he heard her laugh.

Reluctant instinct told him that she was enjoying it, the danger, the knife's edge of possible discovery. Leaving out the obvious pleasure of two males competing for her.

Jersey junk, he reminded himself, that was what she had said about Al Madonna.

And: she thought he was a kind of one-man gang.

Pouring the glass of wine, he looked at the cellar door and then up at the ceiling, his stomach muscles knotted with pain and tension.

For God's sake, Ma, don't wake up with him down here.

Them.

And: spray away, Parker and Parelli, keep it up, in the cellar, don't cut the job short and come asking in front of a witness how that poor lady is now.

He looked at the wall phone.

Mentally, he took the receiver off and dialed the house on Morton Street.

"Dad? Would you come and . . . pick both of us up? Right away? I'll explain when I see you—I don't know what got into me but—"

Crazy.

From the dining room, Mouse's voice called, "Are you stamping on the grapes to get his wine ready for him, Rob?"

He put the wineglass down on the coffee table in front of Al. Al took a quarter from his pocket and laid it on the table. "Thanks, waiter," he said.

Rob wanted to leap on him, but then he thought the noise might go up to the cupola room.

He picked up the coin and gave it to Mouse. "You took his order, you ought to get this."

Mouse closed her hand over it. "Thanks. I never refuse money."

"Money," Al said, sipping his wine. "Money—do I smell it in the air around here?" His eyes on Mouse were half teasing, possessive. "Are you two waiting for a shipment of something? From Mexico or somewhere? I don't see you, Mouse, hanging around for more than a day or so in Prudence, N.J., with just anyone. People can sleep anywhere."

The radio on the table at his elbow was on, low; a rock station. He looked at his watch.

"Time for the news. I always listen, just in case someone's caught up with someone."

Lebanon, a hundred dead. A nursing-home fire, eight dead, ten severely burned and on the critical list. Boy drowned off Barnegat Light. A hijacking in Peru, Pan Am 747. And now a word . . . The announcer had just gotten started on a remedy for something he described as jock itch when Al turned the radio down again.

"Same old crap," he said. "It could have been last month, or even January. Doesn't anybody ever try anything new?"

He had noticed their intensity, listening to the three o'clock news. There was some kind of secret about this house, he sensed, and about their being here.

Were they hiding someone? Waiting for someone? Hiding *from* someone?

Where and how did the police come into their country outing?

The Devore kid looking sick, as if he'd just been kicked in the stomach.

Finishing his wine, he thought, I would like to be around here when they don't know I'm around here.

Figure that out later. Enjoy the moment, get all the juice out of it.

He patted the sofa cushion beside him. "Yeah, fond recollections. Gloomy old place, though. Am I right that the bathroom's opposite the landing upstairs?"

"This isn't a gas station," Rob said.

"Funny, I thought I was a guest. And anyway, it's not your house, it's Mouse's aunt's." He added solemnly, "God rest her soul," and got up and walked into the hall and up the stairs.

He paused on the landing, putting out feelers. Listening. Prodding, sifting, weighing the atmosphere that surrounded him. The house was very quiet. Either they were whispering, in the living room, or not saying anything at all.

Just staring at each other, thinking, how can we get rid of him, before—

There were footsteps, and Rob came up the stairs. "Lost the bathroom? I want it after you."

"Guided tour. Thanks, I know where it is, I was just looking at the view. Some kind of big blue bird out there squawking. Nice pine trees, they make it dark, though. Like I said, gloomy."

"Spruces," Rob said carefully.

He looked at Al's heavily black-haired bronzed arms in the short-sleeved silk shirt. Memorial Couch. Fond recollections. Mouse. His partner and what some nut might now call his, well, fate.

Al in turn studied him. For the first time it occurred to him that maybe this kid had done something naughty, and the reason the police were hunting Mouse was that she was suspected or known to be with Rob Devore. Find her and you'll find him.

He told himself with indignant contempt: But, hell, he probably doesn't know enough ropes to get himself into real, big trouble, police-search trouble. It costs money to send out a wave of men spreading nets.

Well, maybe and maybe not. It didn't pay to underestimate, and that crack about plenty of sleep could be affecting his judgment. Still, a conspiracy, more likely, Mouse wasn't one to be sitting on the sidelines merely watching the action.

One thing was sure. He'd find out what it was all about, before he left Prudence.

14

Mouse whispered to Rob, before he went up the stairs, "Go after him, he can't be allowed to roam the house, wait till he's out of the bathroom, I'll call him. You go on up to your mother."

Her eyes had a strange dark sparkle. "She could wake at any minute, shout or ring that damned bell—"

She waited at the foot of the stairs for the sound of the toilet flushing and the door opening.

"Hey, Al, I've poured you another glass of wine."

"Thanks for the hospitality—seeing you said that it's a private party."

He was aware of being regarded for some reason as a kind of ticking unexploded bomb, and enjoyed it.

She sat beside him on the sofa with her glass of milk. "Speaking of necks of woods, what brought you down to Jersey?"

He had to be gotten rid of, and soon, but she didn't want to antagonize him openly. He had told her with relish some of the things he had done to people who crossed him, or got in his way.

And she had to find out if some instinct of his was asking questions in his head about them, and their presence in this house.

Al explained his visit offhandedly. "Well, I'm back and I wanted *you* back, no mystery about it. This was just one of the places where I was going to look for you, when I heard you were out of town."

"Who told you I was out of town?" Casual question; sedate sip of milk.

"Your roommate, or one of them."

She gave him, for Mouse, a wide smile. "I'm not like your horse, Al, you know," she said. "I don't exactly take to the bit and bridle."

"Neither did Daybreak, at first," Al said. "Raised hell about it."

He felt the tension, the excitement simmering in this usually cooled-down girl, and he decided to make use of it, tease her. Serious investigation could come along in its own time. This was fun.

"So what have you been up to?" He let that hang, and then added, "While I've been away."

Her lashes dropped as she looked into her glass of milk. "What anyone else is up to. Things. Getting around. Passing the time."

"I was so bound and determined to find you I even called his"—he jerked a thumb toward the ceiling—"old man." He remembered how H. L. Devore of Morton Street had sounded, out of kilter one way or another. And that he, like the policeman at the Clipjoint, had been interested in learning Mouse's last name.

He drank off half a glass of his wine. "And what's your little boy doing upstairs? It's ten minutes since he took over the john."

Mouse looked vague. "Maybe napping. We had a late night, last night, a party."

"And baby needs his sleep. I guess you don't want to tell me"—he paused to finish his wine—"what you've gotten yourself into."

Mouse looked him in the eye and said, "Your mind only

works one way, Al. Some people, you know, do just plain have picnics at their aunt's house. God rest her soul, as you say."

He saw that she had clamped down on the simmer and was thoroughly in charge of herself, even enjoying this. Nothing more to be learned, at the moment.

Time was something he never wasted for very long. You could be turning a dollar if you were on your feet. He felt caught in the midafternoon hush of a summer day, a time that gave the impression that nothing ever happened or ever was going to happen.

"Well, Mouse, thanks for whatever this was." He put his glass down. "Enjoy yourself with little Blue-eyes. Be careful not to tire him out. When do I expect you back in town?"

Don't give him the schedule, don't give him anything to go on, he'll work on it.

"Rob will be back tomorrow but I guess *that* doesn't give you the old thrill," she said. "I have to take a quick run to East Hampton, and then Fairfield, but I'll be back, let's see— Sunday, I'll save you Sunday."

"All day Sunday, and straight from there," Al said. He took her in his arms and gave her a hard deep kiss, and walked lightly out into the hall and out the front door.

Rob sat in the church-dim stained light and watched his mother.

Having no desire to participate in her own existence right now, she slept, miles and years away.

He waited for the fist on the door.

The shouted "Hey, what goes on here?"

He found himself totally unable to think, plan, prepare. A phrase of his father's kept repeating itself in his head. There goes the ball game. There goes . . .

Far below, he heard a car door slam. He went over and looked out.

Al Madonna was standing beside the driver's window of the van, talking to an invisible Jimmy Parker.

Then, any minute now, he'll turn around and come back up the porch steps, Rob thought. And into the hall, and up the first flight, and up the second flight.

The van drove off. In the space of perhaps thirty long breaths Al's white Chevrolet convertible followed it down the drive. Gone.

Impossibly, gone away.

Al was coming down the porch steps as Jimmy Parker rounded the corner of the house, his air compressor and a sinister-looking lumpy sack slung over his shoulder. He put both burdens into the back of the van and went to the driver's door.

"Hi, fella," Al said. "How's the bug business?"

Jimmy Parker didn't much like this question from the immaculately white-clad man. What line of work did you have to be in, to be free on a summer afternoon in the middle of the week?

This guy must own the convertible parked at the side of the house. He had been going to say, before Al's greeting, "I see the nut didn't go off in *your* car."

Instead, getting into the van, he said, "It wasn't bugs, it was rats."

"Crazy kind of setup here, isn't it?" Al asked, his bright dark eyes glistening with inquiry.

"No crazier than anywhere else in this town," Jimmy Parker said. "I gotta run." He turned the ignition key.

Photographs of Robert and Madeline Devore were transmitted to police monitors in New Jersey, New York, Delaware, Pennsylvania, and Connecticut. They were accompanied by detailed descriptions of the two, and a description of Mouse culled from Jane's impressions. Long dark hair, dark eyes, late teens, above medium height, thin, no distinguishing marks.

A state policeman in New Haven, Connecticut, said to his

sergeant, "The long dark hair could be blond by now. Or red, or lavender. And they all look alike."

As in all well-conducted kidnapping cases, absolute secrecy was ordained. If the Devores and/or the girl (nickname Mouse, no surname yet available) were spotted, they were not to be directly approached but kept under tight surveillance.

Late in the afternoon the FBI found, in Princeton, New Jersey, the girl Rob Devore had been living with last winter. She was a little annoyed, because her present partner, a senior mathematics major, was expected home soon and he didn't know about Rob. "None of this will come out, will it?" "Absolutely not, as long as you keep to your side of it, you haven't talked to us, you've never seen us." "What has he done, run away?" "Something like that." She had never heard of any girl named Mouse, she hadn't seen Rob since he dropped out. "I mean, not even a card. But he can pretty well take his pick." Did she know of any trouble he'd been in, in college, with the police maybe, that his family wouldn't have been told about? No. "He has, you know, class," she said. "And his father's well known, the architect, not that that has anything to do with anything, but he ran with the okay people." It was one of the hundred blank walls they would run into.

Walter Titus, at the Devore house, was acting as a combination morale upholder, gatekeeper, and telephone answering service. And more importantly as a companion and stay during the long hours.

Mrs. Boland called up in friendly innocence at two and asked if Jane would like to go with her and Elizabeth to the Metropolitan Museum, or was Jane needed at home? Not liking Jane's looks, he said, "Yes, go, after all nothing's going to happen today, nothing at all."

At three, Titus said, "No wonder I hear noises from inside me. I've had no lunch. Have you?"

"There's a sandwich Jane made me but—"

Titus, who did his own cooking, and did it very well, made

two cheese omelettes and broiled a couple of tomatoes powdered with curry. "Come on, sit down, stop prowling, I can't eat if you won't. Is there any white wine chilled?"

At Devore's stare, he said, "Sanity is sometimes a matter of going on, outwardly, as if everything is all right. Ah, good man," as Devore poured wine.

Devore thought it was indecent that, bitterly frightened as he was, he was hungry. They ate their omelettes in silence. Titus handled a phone call in mid-tomato. A girl for Rob, breathless pretty voice, "I just got in from Holland, is he there?" "No, sorry, let me have your name." Her name was Sally Fisher. "I thought after I snatched an hour or so of sleep I'd have a party and see people, will you tell him, please, eight o'clock?" "I'll tell him."

While he was making the coffee, Titus asked, "Does Madeline keep any kind of diary? Places where she might go when you were away that he—they—might know about and have some kind of entrance to? A quarrel or threat she'd kept from you so as not to worry you? Or maybe something about that girl Mouse, she may have been quite often to the house even if Jane only saw her once, Jane's just now out of school . . ."

Madeline did keep daybooks. This year's was one she had bought at the Tate Gallery in London, scattered through with reproductions of Turner watercolors. She liked to put in weather, so she could compare one spring or summer with another; she was a great enjoyer and collector of weather.

And she put in oddments from books she was reading that she wanted to remember. And trenchant witty bits and pieces of Tom Wicker, Russell Baker, Anthony Lewis, from her morning browsings over the *Times*.

She kept it on the white writing desk in their bedroom. Devore, who never before would have dreamed of touching it, picked it up with reluctant fingers and began reading, turning the pages back from June 9.

It was eerily like being alone with her, alone and in close physical contact.

He scanned the small stylish handwriting a little guiltily and at great speed. A space of about an inch and a half was ruled off for each day. A few were blank.

"Frightful wind today, the city's absolutely rocking . . . Letter from H., from Toronto, home tomorrow thank God, remember to make corn bread . . . hot, humid, high 80's, sunny-cloudy . . . Jane sick in bed with a virus . . . Brendan Behan when he was dying said in gratitude to his nurse, who was a nun, 'May all your sons be bishops . . .' Three new hanging baskets, put them on the garden wall . . . Scene between Rob and H. almost knocked the house down . . ."

Wanting her presence, feeling it near, he went hungrily on, back. "Put the cosmos in . . . wrote H. something ridiculously like a love letter . . ." He remembered the letter. He was badly shaken by the words, the woman, coming up at him from the dove-gray pages.

And: H., H., H., H. His moods, though rare, keenly noted and lightly recorded. "H. very dark last night, a thunderstorm and then a nice clearing; the Colorado library." A splendid chalk-striped gray vested suit had been delivered. "H. tried it on and asked me, he is at his most endearing when he is anxious, did he look too much like the Chase Manhattan Bank, and I said no, he looked marvelous in it . . ." "H. as always says he is immune to colds but has an awful one and went uptown anyway." His arrivals, his departures. A night when he hadn't been able to sleep. Celebrations, presents. "H. got up at one and said, 'How would you like a glass of champagne?'" . . . "H. brought me an Hermès scarf from Toronto, with the Arms of Paris on it, and a lovely old *Pickwick Papers* in ivory leather . . ."

He made himself go back to March and then closed the ring-bound notebook. Nothing, nothing at all here but Madeline Devore. Her days, her world, her husband, seen from a vantage point of safety and love.

When he came downstairs Titus looked away from his contained stricken face and was glad to be able to say, "I think you'd better telephone your office. A young man named Lederer called wanting to know when you'd be back. He sounded upset about something."

Devore Associates was largely speaking a one-man show. Devore did not take kindly to collaboration, compromise, and committees. The big ideas were his ideas, their power and shape and clarity undimmed by the business of putting heads together, reacting to the reactions of others. He employed talented young men to see to the necessary drudgery, the underpinnings. It was well worth it to them; they were pleasantly paid and a job with Devore was a sought-after professional plum. Nowhere to go, after your stint there, but up.

Lederer's problem was a plumbers' strike in Wilmington, where the Mariners Life Insurance tower was going up. "I thought you ought to know . . ." Devore was a stickler about keeping to schedules; his buildings usually met their deadlines, which was rare in this business. "I assume you'll be in tomorrow, but I thought I'd check with Mrs. Devore to make sure."

Devore said they'd make up time somewhere else and that, no, he wouldn't be in tomorrow. Maybe Friday, possibly late Friday.

He was, because of his initials, referred to behind his back by certain members of his staff as Hell. "Funny," Lederer said, turning from the phone to the man at the next drawing board, "Hell didn't sound like himself. Dithery, sort of. I suppose that flight from Tokyo's enough to knock anyone cold."

Al Madonna thought it might be wise to do a little scouting through the underbrush before moving straight ahead.

It occurred to him that the police might be interested in Mouse simply because her parents were for some reason hunting her. Her telephone number was an unlisted one and she used a post office box number to pick up her monthly check from them. Maybe something had happened in the family, someone dead or something, and they wanted their dear little Margaret home. He gathered from things Mouse had idly dropped that they were rich; the police did nice, obliging errands for the rich.

Prudence was a blank as far as services and conveniences for the general public went. He drove to the nearest decent-sized town, Newton, went to the telephone company office and requested a directory for Fairfield County, Connecticut.

There were two Astons listed in Greenwich. Aston, G. G., and Aston, Thomas A., Mrs., for all he knew, the grandmother. G. G. looked right. He went into a booth and dialed.

Mrs. Gordon Aston had just returned from the hairdresser's. They had made a nice soft, short, loose job of her hair and a nap wouldn't hurt it. She spread a light veil of Revlon Eterna Cream over her face, stripped, and got into bed. Three delicious dozy hours before she met Gordon for drinks and dinner at the club, with those attractive new people, the Merritts.

The maid put her head in at the door after knocking. "Phone, Mrs. Aston, a Mr. Finch, says it's important."

Swearing softly, Mrs. Aston turned her phone back on. An unfamiliar voice, and to her ear a rather uneducated one, male, said confidentially, "If you're looking for Mouse, I think I know where you can find her."

Mrs. Aston said in astonishment, "Looking for *Mouse?* Why on earth should we be looking for Mouse? It's the other way around. If she wants us, she knows where to find us. But, thank you, anyway," and she hung up.

"You should learn to have a better control of your face," Mouse said severely to Rob. "Any fool looking at you could tell you had your hand in some kind of cookie jar. Not that he's a fool. We were lucky we got rid of him so easily."

She paused, considered, and added on a long expelled breath, "I don't even like to *think* about what could have happened."

15

"Jane, dear, aren't you well?" asked kind Mrs. Boland.

After seeing the Degas exhibition at the Metropolitan, they had gone across Fifth Avenue to the Stanhope Hotel. Mrs. Boland was having a gin and tonic and the girls were drinking iced tea.

Miss Minnott's School, where both Jane and Elizabeth went —the Devores believed in tough, steep, demanding education —had an eighty-year-old program of summer projects for their girls. Just, they said at Miss Minnott's, to keep the mind from going completely on holiday.

Jane excelled in art class and one of the ten projects on her list was a detailed report of a visit to a museum.

She hadn't properly taken in anything that she looked at, although it was all dreamily lovely. She kept seeing and hearing instead the oddest things.

Police feet, responding to Mr. Titus's call, tramping busily through the house in Greens Farms, the safe white house under its maples. Looking everywhere, including her own yellow and white room with its sleigh bed and dimity café curtains, looking for Rob, looking for her mother.

And Rob, Rob at twelve when she was going on six and had naturally worshipped him, Rob swaying upright, dangerously, at the top of the tallest sycamore on the lawn. Daring Rob, nothing he wouldn't attempt. He had once tried to get down the angled chimney from the rooftop and had to be gone after by the fire department and pried out. Blue and golden Rob, haughtily nice to the annoying kid following on his heels.

Sirens screaming, after Rob. But no, they'd have to be silent, the police cars, hunting him, hunting her mother . . . they'd have to be secret.

Mrs. Boland took another sip of her drink and saw goose pimples texture Jane's lightly tanned arms in her gray linen sleeveless dress. The thick radiant skin of her face had a faint blue tinge.

"My mother—" she said before she could stop herself.

"Yes, dear? Madeline—?"

Jane desperately wanted to tell, and share it, and have a warm blanket of amazement and sympathy spread over her. After all, the Bolands were their friends, her mother and Mrs. Boland were always in and out of each other's gardens—

Mrs. Boland would say, "But that's nonsense, Rob couldn't possibly have—" But Mrs. Boland had at least twenty friends, and her younger brother worked for one of the news weeklies.

To give herself time, she took the thin lemon slice from the edge of her glass and ate it; as always, the taste brought tears to her eyes.

"I think Mother would like to see the Degas exhibition," she said.

Halligan, having had all the coffee he could drink and more, took a breather from the Clipjoint in the late afternoon and went up Bleecker Street and cleansed his palate with several beers.

He was just in time, when he got back, to hear a tow-haired boy with a sunburn ask the waitress, "Mouse been in?"

Halligan informally joined him at the little table. "Hey, I'm looking for her too." He got the white envelope out of his pocket.

"He's sort of neat," the waitress said to the girl at the espresso machine, "but he's queer for birthday cards."

"Freshen my memory, how to spell her last name?"

"Ashton," the boy said. "I think. Everybody just calls her Mouse."

"I've looked around and she doesn't seem to be in town. Maybe visiting her parents or something?"

The boy laughed. "You're kidding."

"But she used to talk about the old homestead in that way of hers . . . where was it again?"

"Some fancy Connecticut town—Westport, maybe. Or Ridgefield?" The boy lifted his arm in a wave to someone coming in at the door, and got up and left the table.

Ashton, I think. Westport, maybe.

Halligan ordered a cappuccino after he had made his unpromising telephone call.

An extensive police check began immediately to follow up this lead, the wrong name in two wrong towns.

White's no good, Al Madonna thought. Too visible. I'd shine in the dark like a goddam glowworm.

He went into an Army and Navy supply store in Newton and bought a pair of cheap black cotton trousers and a large-pocketed blue denim jacket. No hemming and hawing about sizes, no try-ons or anything to make him remembered as a customer.

He thought about changing his clothes in the men's room at the bus station and rejected the idea. Go in dressed one way, come out another, someone might recall it. My trouble is, I catch people's eye, he reminded himself complacently. Better to pull off into a lane, and change in the car.

He was equipped and ready now. Gun and knife in the dashboard compartment of the Chevrolet. All he needed was the absence of daylight. If they were up to something, they'd be watching, and not just the drive. That is, if they had the sense.

Amateurs, Al thought, should never tangle with the pros.

"Go to sleep, Rob," Mouse said. "You look like a television commercial for sleeping stuff. I mean, you look like before, not after."

He had been sitting thinking. Like the old man said, I could have been playing a piano in the Catskills. "You do that very well." Girls, singles, hanging over his piano, flirting and buying him drinks.

Or getting a tan with a road gang, hard innocent work, ice-cold beer when you got a break.

But instead, he was landed with this. It had been some kind of sheer cliff to scale, to show his father, to prove something—

From years ago, he heard his mother murmur at the breakfast table, "God save us from people who want to prove something . . . hone their knives against you."

He got up from his chair and went to her Aunt Grace's old Baldwin upright and started playing. "I Never Promised You a Rose Garden." He didn't like the implications of that and stopped after two bars. The garden at the back of the house. Jane's plump little sculptured penguin sitting in the middle of the white table under the ash tree.

Jane was good with her hands, she had sculptured a head of him as a ten-year-old, from a photograph; he was ashamed of being so pleased and flattered about it and had hidden it in his bottom bureau drawer.

What would Jane think of—?

His room, his bureau, his records . . . what was it like now, back there on Morton Street? He saw the way the late slanting sunlight came into the dining room through the hanging baskets, and heard the kitchen sounds, a broiler pan being pulled out, the small crash of an ice tray having its aluminum bones jerked out as his father got drinks for himself and Ma. Music on, not his kind of music, classical stuff . . .

Last year he had feasted for a short time on his father's vintage jazz records. Now he began with able violent fingers on the "St. Louis Blues."

The out-of-tune piano cried rage and grief to the dark red-curtained room. Its sound went through the windows to the weeping spruces and the silent overgrown meadowy lawns.

Mouse, suddenly and badly disturbed, came over and sat down on the piano seat beside him.

"Great, Rob, *great*, but do you want to wake the dead?"

"The what?" He stopped playing. His eyes looking into hers were enormous and bluer than she had ever seen them.

From high above, there came the sound of a bell.

"Oh God, she's awake," Mouse said. "Time to walk the dog. To the bathroom, that is."

Rob turned on the piano bench and brought up his arm and struck her across the face with the flat of his palm. She almost fell backward but saved herself by clutching the keyboard.

Then she struck him back, her fist clenched, an impact like a flung stone in the center of his forehead.

He gave a small bewildered shake of his head and before he could collect himself she was off the bench and out of the room. She came back in with the gun, pointed at him in a speaking manner.

"From the Al Madonnas, yes, that's a sort of way of making love, with them. From you, no," Mouse said softly. "You're a nice well-brought-up boy."

She aimed and fired; at first Rob didn't know what her hand was doing, what the unbelievable ringing crashing noise was. The bullet deliberately missed his left foot by ten inches and made a small discreet black hole in the green-flowered dark red rug before it buried itself in depths of wood and stone underneath.

"Just so you know what you're up against," Mouse said when the shocking echoes had died away. "I always thought *you* didn't think this was loaded, but just a, kind of, prop. Well, you see, it is. Loaded, I mean."

Madeline, sitting on the edge of her bed, heard the terrible destroying noise and cried out and failed to hear her own cry, with that crash against her ears.

She folded her arms about herself, head bent almost to her knees. She tried to pray but her mind was a white blank. Oh God, was all she could manage in the circumstances, oh God, oh God, oh God—

Knowing it was useless, she got up and flung herself against the door, wrenching at the knob.

On a ripped sobbing breath, she cried, "*Rob—*" A voice just outside the door said, "Coming, Ma, it's all right," and the door opened and the two of them came in. No wounds, no blood. Intact.

Mouse spoke first, Miss Porter's again, after a glance at the white face. Madeline put a hand to her lips, which were shaking; she never remembered having this special visible tremor before.

"Sorry about the commotion," Mouse said. "Actually Rob and I had a little difference of opinion and you know how, in old movies—westerns—they shoot the light out, or fire at a glass of whiskey, to show how good their aim is? Just to prove their point."

Madeline found nothing to say to this. She looked at Rob and he looked at her hands, her shoulder, anywhere but into her eyes.

One way or another, poor Rob is in bad shape, she thought, and then couldn't help a faint sound that might have been laughter, or hysteria, or a little of both.

"Thieves falling out," she said.

She watched the color come up hot and red under Rob's skin. When he was younger, much younger, the rush of red meant that he was about to burst into a storm of tears.

"Shall we be off to the ladies'?" Mouse suggested.

Thank God her legs weren't shaking, now. They went down to the bathroom on the half-landing, she preceding Mouse.

This quiet mad girl might very possibly shoot me in the back, right now, right on this step, or this one. She's in command here.

Her ears and the muscles of her back waited for another near and final crash.

"No tricks with towels, Mrs. Devore," Mouse said gently.

"No tricks with towels. Now that you've made your point, with that."

Rob was sitting on the stairs, waiting, when they came out of the bathroom. Madeline found it extremely odd that her first impression was that he was there, not a dozen feet from the door, to guard her.

"It's almost cocktail hour, Ma," he said. "What would you like?"

"Robert in Wonderland," replied his mother.

"No, I mean it. You still look shook. I found half a bottle of gin under the sink, in the cupboard with the soap powder and stuff, maybe the cook if there was one sneaked a drink. I can make you almost a martini, maybe a little Chablis in it, after all Dad uses a dash of sherry when he's out of vermouth—"

"That," Madeline said politely, "would be very nice, Rob."

When Madeline's cocktail had been delivered to her, with an extra one in a tarnished silver shaker, and the door had been bolted, Mouse said, "Friends again?" and put out her hand to him.

He made himself clasp it. "Yes, sure, Mouse."

"Good. Because we have to have a nice sensible talk, see where we are, sort of. Why don't you get yourself a beer while I make some lemonade."

They took their drinks into the living room and sat down side by side on the sofa. It was time for the five o'clock news. Bus hit by a tractor-trailer on the New Jersey Turnpike, thirty-five injured, one dead, the driver. "Don't bother straining your ears," Mouse interrupted in the middle of an account of a bridge collapsing in Florence, into the Arno, casualties had yet to be estimated— "If it was about us, we'd be what they call the top of the news. I mean, what's bigger news than a son kidnapping his own mother? And your father's reputation and all."

With the weather, she took a thoughtful sip of her lemonade. Cloudy, increasing humidity tonight with a forty percent possibility of rain, heavy rains tomorrow . . .

"There's a forty percent possibility that you might screw this whole thing up," Mouse said. "Which is what we're going to talk about."

Rob had never before had to, consciously, act a role. He had taken for granted all his life the luxury of feeling and thinking and saying exactly what you wanted to.

Now, invisibly, he put on his stage makeup and picked up his script and began to read it.

"What exactly does that mean, Mouse?"

"You're getting cold feet and second thoughts." She shook her glass vigorously. "Sugar's all down at the bottom. . . . Your dear darling ma. It was crazy and fun at first, you were a sort of Columbus—"

"*We* were," Rob cut softly in.

"She's your mother, not mine. In case you haven't thought it all the way through, here it is. If you try to do something to me, and let her get away, or take her away, it will all have been for nothing. All the both of us will have to look forward to is a lot of years behind bars. Men raping you and women raping me, and things. Roaches and dirty mattresses and not enough toilets to go around. Don't kid yourself that someone hasn't called the police into it."

Again, that strange sparkle in her eyes; a feeding on danger, on brinks.

"Go on, Mouse," he said. "Continue the forty percent lecture."

She gave him a surprised glance. His blue eyes were cool and his proper rose-golden color was back. He took a long drink of his beer with what seemed perfectly simple thirst and pleasure.

"Okay. On the one hand this, on the other hand that. We

stick to it. Your father sticks to his side of it, anyone with a grain of sense would, considering what—"

She left that hanging.

He heard again the sound of her gun and saw the little burned black hole in the rug, under the piano bench.

"Well, on the other hand, the *nice* hand—she's free and safe, we're free and safe, and loaded." Mouse contemplated a lemon pit she had just lightly removed from her tongue. "Midstream is a lousy place to be, but to me the far bank ahead of us looks a whole lot better."

"Quite a flight, Mouse," Rob said lazily.

"You sound nice when you're Rob again. As for the flight, I always, back then, got straight A's in English composition."

"I assume you'll put the gun back on the counter?"

"Yes, for both of us, now we're all squared away. We are, aren't we?"

"Of course, idiot," Rob said. "Full speed ahead, to your far bank. When you think about it, 'bank' is the right word, isn't it?"

". . . and just to show you my heart is in the right place, I'll clean up the kitchen. *When* are you going to sleep?"

"Sooner or later." He handed her his empty beer can in a lordly way. "You might bring me another while you're on your feet."

She did, and with it she brought crackers and cheese, which he looked at and knew he couldn't possibly eat.

Faint domestic sounds reached his ears from the kitchen. Water running, glass clinking against china, the hinged lid of the garbage can dropping back into place.

Sitting on his spine on the sofa, legs stretched out, he closed his eyes for a few minutes' rest from now, from Ma, and Mouse, and fell down deep into a tremendous consuming sleep.

16

Al Madonna parked his car deep in a lane across and down
the road from the Aston place. He pulled it well off the rutted
dirt, under a weeping willow tree.

Rich purple June twilight enfolded him. Just enough light
to see by, and it wouldn't last much longer. The night noises
were peaceful, a breeze stirring the leaves and grass, a chuck-
ling sort of bird note, a jet plane far overhead. He hoped
there weren't snakes around. There were very few things that
frightened him, but snakes were among them. Weren't there
copperheads in Jersey? Probably not here, though, with all
these rich people around; they wouldn't tolerate them.

He went in through the main gates, slipped behind the
rhododendron hedge to his left, and keeping to its dark looming shelter, followed it up the drive.

A few cracks of light from the living room, where the curtains didn't quite meet. No lights in the front hall or on the
porch. Illuminated dim green and a purple just a shade paler
than the twilight, at the top of one of those crazy wooden
towers. Funny, you'd expect more of a blaze; that pair didn't
look as if they were worried about conserving electricity to
help out in the energy crisis.

Close against the house walls, he went around to the back.
Lights on here, at the center, in the kitchen, a double fluores-

cent bar on the white ceiling. There were two windows with opaque white sash curtains just a few inches higher than his eye level, with above them flowered blue and white curtains looped back.

Almost immediately he spotted the missing pane in the kitchen door, its glass tidily removed, no jags to cut yourself on. He drew the correct inference: this wasn't a kosher visit to dear old dead Auntie's, they had broken in.

He could see shadows moving indistinctly, dark beyond the crisp white curtains. And more importantly, through the empty oblong in the door, he could hear their voices.

He stood with his back against the house wall, to the right of the kitchen step, and listened.

Mouse. "Oh God, we forgot ketchup. How I'm ever to get my french fries down—" Al heard her yawn.

"Try Worcestershire, it's good on them, there's a big bottle of it in the cupboard."

"She didn't eat very much, and seeing the trouble you went to you might as well eat up her salad."

"She." Al garnered the pronoun and put it in his pocket.

"Light the oven, will you, it says four hundred degrees on the package. . . . Too bad you lost your spell in bed, it's my turn again, soon, but honest to God you looked like a dead man on the sofa, I had to call you four times."

"Your spell." One up, one down. Guard duty.

"Is this hamburger or dog food? It's full of fat."

Mouse laughed. "You're spoiled rotten. I have to admit she's a good cook."

Al listened, spine pressing the house wall; braced, dark, and dangerous.

"If you broil it, some of the fat will drip out. It's funny she doesn't scream, of course nobody but us could have heard it from the cellar but I don't know about up there . . ."

"You said there are six acres and it must be at least a quarter of a mile to the gate."

"Yes, and there aren't ever many cars along Bellamy Road,

and this place *is* supposed to be haunted. It would be nicer if we had just the one day to get through and not two . . ."

Sizzling broiling sounds. A light smell of grease from the french-fried potatoes heating in the oven. Noises of plates being set down, knives, forks, spoons.

She, Al thought. Unwilling compliment from Mouse: "I have to admit she's a good cook." Former girl friends didn't invite current girl friends to dinner, with or without the male involved.

And so far, *she* hadn't tried screaming, because she'd probably been told no one would hear her, why bother?

They had, for some reason, a prisoner here in this house. What would a couple of kids want with a prisoner, a woman?

The screech of a broiler pan. "Oh God, it's burned . . ."

"Ketchup would have kind of drowned out the black, too bad, but there's mustard up there, and relish."

Al started slightly as an owl hooted in a tree somewhere near. From nowhere, a cat appeared in the dim light that came through the curtains and wove itself about his ankles, rubbing and purring. He wanted to kick it away but it might yowl. The purring was loud in his ears. Could they possibly hear it, in there?

Lured by the smell of meat and grease, the cat jumped up onto the kitchen step and began meowing vociferously. Probably lived off mice and things in the woods and was hungry, Al thought, as with a lightning quiet he moved along the wall and around the corner of the house.

He heard the kitchen door open. "Well, what do you know, a cat," Mouse said. "Poor thing, its sides are all caved in."

What if the cat ran away from her and back to him and Mouse followed it?

She said over her shoulder to Rob, "Shall I let it in? Cats have always been good luck to me."

"What if it's not housebroken?"

"They're clean, they learn fast. I'll fix a carton with newspapers torn up in it. It's really kind of a pretty cat . . ."

"Is that a good idea, when you have to abandon it again?"

"At least," Mouse said, "it will have had one whole night and one whole day of fancy living. I'll give it milk and a nice little dish of your dog meat. Here, kitty, good kitty . . ." The cat must have responded; there was the sound of the kitchen door closing.

For Christ's sake, Al thought, cats and ketchup and french fries, get on with it, will you?

He moved back to his position close to the door. They must finally be sitting down at the table; chairs scraped and their voices were coming from the far side of the room.

With her mouth half full of something, Mouse laughed. "After all," she said, "if you can spoil your mother I can spoil my cat."

There was a peculiar ringing in Al's ears, and a tingle in his fingertips which he was able to identify as shock, an odd sensation for him.

His own father was dead but his mother was very much and very volubly alive, in Vineland, New Jersey. She disapproved of him and of his way of life, about which she had strong suspicions, but through her showers of scolding her adoration burned clearly and permanently.

He liked to give her presents when he'd pulled a little something off, perfume, a topaz ring once, a good expensive fake fur coat because she felt the cold in winter.

"Ill-gotten gains," she would cry. "Maybe *hot*, stolen, how would I know?" But after that came a huge warm thanking hug and kiss.

It was the kid's mother—the lord-of-the-manor kid—here in this house. Whose salad had been taken so much trouble over, whose cooking Mouse admitted was good, who hadn't yet tried screaming, who had to be watched, one sleeping and one awake . . .

And H. L. Devore with his raw tired voice, wanting to know Mouse's last name. The policeman at the Clipjoint, inquiring ever so casually about Mouse . . .

"No coffee for me, thanks," Mouse said. She yawned again. "I don't want to wake myself up. Did you eat all the chocolate cupcakes?"

Something was dawning on Al, but he pushed it away.

Right down to his Italian marrow, he could not believe it. He had very few traditional morals and obeyed very few rules, but this, he said, I don't believe.

Pull yourself together, look at it another way, he told himself, figure all the angles. Maybe they haven't taken her *for* something, but *from* something. Maybe she'd been fooling around with other men, and H. L. Devore was out for her blood, had threatened her life. Like his own Uncle Val had, a couple of years ago, and Uncle Val had followed it up and knifed Aunt Gloria in three places before they stopped him. She died anyway.

Maybe the sleeping-waking watch was to be able to spot her husband's car coming up the drive, hellbent. Maybe she hadn't wanted to admit her guilt and run away, and they thought it was best for her, and took her against her will, to keep her safe, to keep her alive.

"Now, about tonight, here's what I thought," Mouse said. "I'll put a footstool in front of the wing chair, for you. If you want to close an eye now and then, it's all right, I'll be sleeping on the sofa right near you."

Silence. Al almost heard Rob Devore's stare.

"What the *hell*—?"

"Your feet might get cold again while I'm asleep." Another little silence, and then, "It's chilly at night here. And I'd rather be around you than alone, up in that big old bedroom . . . I'll bring down blankets for both of us."

Al's taste buds watered at the smell of hot fresh coffee being poured at the stove a few feet away from him.

"Two people to watch over," Rob's voice said, cool. "Me and Ma."

"Well," Mouse said, "we're all in this together. Let's get out of this kitchen. God, it's all dirty again."

Didn't trust him, didn't want to let him out of her sight or away from her side, Al thought. This didn't fit with the rescue idea at all. And somehow he couldn't connect Mouse with daring acts of kindness, and giving up days and nights to help someone else's—anybody's—mother. And why the police, unless Devore had special pull?

On the whole, he was inclined to go back to his first, impossible theory.

They had left the lights on in the kitchen. As he remembered, there was the dining room beyond it, and then the broad hall, with the living room to the right on the far side of the hall. He put his hand in through the empty pane, unlocked the door, stepped into the kitchen and flicked it with his eyes.

The gun on the counter top beside the canister labeled "Coffee" immediately caught his attention.

The pockets of his denim jacket held his own weapons. He picked up the Colt, looked consideringly around, and thrust it deep into the garbage pail, hand demanding a hasty removal from wet stuff, God knows what, and cans and bottles and wads of paper toweling.

It was a valuable and useful object to be disposed of in this manner. But garbage is not collected from untenanted houses, and if and when wanted, could be retrieved.

He went back to his inspection. There was a closed door opposite the back door, next to the open swinging door into the butler's pantry. Cellar, he concluded. Another door to his right, slightly open, showed stairs going up, a narrow boxed-in back stairway.

He left the door its same exact four inches open, behind him, and went up softly and soundlessly on the bare wood. The door at the top was unlocked. It opened into a long wide hall with at the far end a step up to the raised landing at the top of the front stairway. Along the hall, there were four closed doors, two on each side, bedrooms probably. A faint light sifted up from the lower hall.

Mouse had said she'd bring down blankets for them, and

might decide to do her errand any minute now. Nobody had linen closets downstairs, it would have to be up here somewhere.

Normally a man of finger-snapping impatience, Al could find all kinds of patience when it was necessary. He went and stood inside the back stairway, leaving the door open a crack.

In five minutes he saw Mouse on the landing. She opened a tall narrow door across from the bathroom and reached in and got out two blankets, two sheets, and a pillow.

She stood a moment, looking up the second flight of stairs, in a listening attitude. Waiting for the screaming to start, maybe?

Then she turned, chin resting on her armload, and went downstairs.

The listening look upward saved him the time and trouble of checking the four closed doors on this floor; in any case his animal awareness told him there was no one in any of them. He remembered the dim strange-colored light in the windows high up over the roof.

It was very dark when he climbed to the half-landing. He switched on his pencil flash and saw a door there. Too small a space for a bedroom and yes, it was another bathroom. He turned the corner and went up twelve more steep steps, showed himself the white door with its heavy bolt in place, switched off the flash, and stood listening.

"Hail Mary, full of grace," he heard the low voice start.

Madeline was trying to hold firmly on to her sanity. Her own voice, out loud, was a kind of company for her.

She had so far recited two decades of the rosary (the rosary was unfashionable now among well-informed Catholics, but it had a curiously soothing effect, taking you back to childhood safeties and certainties), and Yeats's "Leda and the Swan," and the poem of Emily Dickinson's which began with "I dwell in possibility." Then she went back to the rosary. She didn't own beads anymore; she said it on her fingers, being careful to keep exact count.

If it had only been herself, it might have been more bearable. Hope for the best, wait it out, only one more day.

But it wasn't just herself. She could not, mentally, look into Hugh's face, his eyes, his mind, without an anguished tearing inside her.

Look away from Hugh, you must. The thing was to get from minute to minute, occupation to occupation. Finish her rosary. Set a goal of five, six chapters to be read in one of her paperbacks, and then read one beyond the goal, to coax sleep. Think about Jane, hardy Jane. Had he told her? "But, *Rob . . .* ? I mean, he *couldn't* have . . ." No, don't think about Jane either.

There was a pitcher of cold water and a glass on the bedside table, and Rob had put a little flat metal box of aspirin there too. "In case you have trouble sleeping."

The idea of another attempt at escape had only to be thought of to be rejected. Rob had wired the window latches shut, knotting the wire with his pliers. Even if she could undo the wire, and get out a window, there was the long drop to the roof. Then, you had to get down from the roof to the ground. How? Perhaps a tree, climb down that—but then where would you run to? With Mouse at her heels in all probability, Mouse and her gun. Two unappealing alternatives: a broken neck or back, slipping and falling; or a bullet.

Hugh . . . As before, she said, "I know I'm alive but he doesn't," and then wondered if she had said it aloud, in the middle of her prayer.

She had, and Al Madonna heard it, just before "Give us this day our daily bread and forgive us our trespasses . . ."

The seven half-gasped words made up his mind for him.

What a thing for anyone to do to their mother.

They weren't going to be allowed to get away with it, profit by it themselves.

Not with the victim indecently a part of the family.

An icing of long-ago First Communion outraged innocence bedecked his own plans in white.

17

Mouse finished making up her bed on the sofa. "I want some more milk, will you get it?"

It was nice that she invariably had a nightcap of milk. "Okay, I can use another beer myself."

They had brought along the sleeping pills in case violent resistance required heavy sedation. The bottle was in the kitchen cabinet.

He melted a capsule in hot water and added the liquid to the tall glass of milk. He opened his beer, and it was then that he noticed the gun was missing from the counter.

Rotten lying Mouse. She'd hidden it somewhere.

But in a way he wasn't surprised. It was some time long before this, he couldn't put his finger on exactly when, that he had come to recognize her as the enemy. Someone to match wits with, someone to fight, to conquer, no matter how.

Sleep first, for her. Search for the gun later.

"Are you going to bed in your clothes, like that?"

"I might have to hop up, in the night, and bare-ass and all— I told you, it gets chilly."

Still prepared to watch him. As he would watch her. He gave her her milk and held his breath as she tasted it and scowled.

"I hope that hot dog was all right, my mouth tastes funny." She hesitated, then thirstily gulped the glassful down.

Flipping up the folded sheet, she got in between and lay down on her back, head deep in the pillow in a sprawl of dark hair.

"Turn the light off, Rob? Mine, not yours, and leave the radio on low. Just in case . . ."

"Okay. Night, Mouse." He switched off the lamp on the end table near her head and went and half sat, half lay in the huge ugly dark green upholstered chair at the foot of the sofa.

Mouse—fighting sleep like a child when there is excitement in the air, a party going on in the house—studied through her lashes the golden hair on his long beautifully muscled brown legs, not too much, just enough of it; his half-closed eyes, through which blue could be seen, lamplight catching it; his long strong hands loosely holding the arms of his chair. The golden petals of his new haircut fell thickly around his close-set ears and over his forehead, and were shaping nicely at the base of his neck. He's, well, neat, Mouse thought, I always liked him before but now he's, I don't know, different. Older?

Under his gaze, she fell obviously and totally asleep.

Wait a few minutes, then go upstairs.

Unbolt the door, finger to lips, although Mouse looked now as if she wouldn't wake up if a cannon was fired across the room.

Put on some clothes and shoes quick, Ma, don't bother with the suitcase or the junk. Don't make a sound, Ma.

Softly along the hall to the back stairway, down to the kitchen, out through the darkness to the garage. He wouldn't need a flash or anything, he'd guide her, fast, his feet knew the way.

Jump into the car, and just to be on the extra-safe side, skip the drive. Take the grown-over back lane that led from behind the barn, under a heavy double row of maples, winding through the woods and up a hill and through low gateposts, out onto Farricker Road.

Drive obediently at the speed limit—this wasn't the time to be stopped by the police, any more than when they were taking her away to sell her back to his father—to the bus station. Give her some money, keep her in the car with him until the next bus left for New York.

Maybe she'd forgive him and maybe she wouldn't, but right now it didn't seem to matter.

Get her out, send her back to Morton Street, and his father, and the garden, and Jane.

And come back and face Mouse and say . . . what? Play that part of it by ear, that part of it was ancient history, anyway.

He got up from his chair, did a little close eyelash-watching, and was satisfied. But just in case, he went into the kitchen and took out of a drawer a wood-handled sharp-edged knife of carbon steel with a six-inch blade. He wasn't going to be stopped by her, this time.

The cat had been lying under the kitchen table on a cushion Mouse had taken off the rocker. "I don't want her sleeping with me, the poor thing probably has fleas." A replenished saucer of milk and a bowl of water were beside her; the saucer with the raw remains of his hamburger meat was licked clean. She got up sleepily and rubbed her head against his sneakers. He pushed her softly and kindly away, went back through the dining room into the hall, hesitated about turning off the one dim-watted lamp on the hall desk, decided against it, and started up the broad carpeted stairs.

Al, moving like a dancer to music, conducted himself by the sounds, the comings and goings, the whereabouts of their voices from below.

When Mouse came up to the bathroom, he was invisible on the half-landing above her. Then a little more chitchat from the living room, radio on, rock, somebody snarling, "Baby I hate you because baby I love you." Al preferred classical music and opera.

She wanted milk. He'd have a beer.

He went to the top of the back stairway and listened to the refrigerator door opening and closing, the hiss of the beer being opened, a glass held under the tap, a spoon tinkling in it, stirring. A return to the front end of the hall. "Leave the radio on low . . ." "Night, Mouse."

Al waited patiently. The silence was profound under the whisper of the radio. No crackling of a newspaper, no striking of a match to light a cigarette. Had the kid gone to sleep too, in his chair?

He didn't want one of them in one room and one maybe in the kitchen, coming up behind him.

His feet were beginning to ache, standing still like this. Then, after the creak of a spring, the dancer moved to his place at the top of the back stairway. A drawer opening, shutting, a click as the ceiling fluorescents were switched off. Still a little light down there, there must be one lamp burning.

If you want to keep this up all night, Al thought, I'll keep it up, right along with you. The moment when it came would show itself loud and clear.

It did.

Several minutes later he saw Rob carefully close the living-room door and start up the stairs.

Al, coming down, met him at the halfway point.

18

"Hi, there." Very softly.

Al Madonna had almost every advantage over Rob.

He was two steps higher on the stairway when ascent and descent came to a standstill and they looked at each other.

Another advantage was shock, blue eyes returning a stunned stare to the dark lively gaze.

A third was the held-in violence implicit in the braced tough body facing him, above him. It suggested, the body, experience with the administering of injury.

Al suddenly had a knife in his hand, fist near his chest, blade outward, the dim light from the hall desk catching the edge of it. There was no doubt that he would know, exactly and instantly, what to do with the knife.

"Keep your knee down, if that's what's in your head," he said, his voice low and almost conversational. "It wouldn't work but if you tried I'm not sure where I'd get you, with this."

If Mouse were awake and listening, she could have by now gone for her gun, wherever it was, or thrown something at Al's head, but he had put Mouse effectively and deeply to sleep.

"No point in waking her," Al murmured as if reading his mind. "Turn around, dining room, let's talk."

Was this the way his mother had felt, Mouse behind her

with the gun? Not knowing at which portion of a second someone might casually and in final tearing pain obliterate you?

He walked slowly, very upright, two feet ahead of Al into the dining room. Al touched a wall switch and the Tiffany glass lamp hanging five feet above the table came on, irises and lilies, violets and twining green ivy leaves, a blossomy light falling on the long bare mahogany surface. He reached behind him and closed the door, as thick and heavy as the door into the living room, dark golden paneled oak.

Standing against it, he said, "Inspection time, you never know." Knife point several inches from Rob's throat, he felt in the pockets of the cutoff gray flannel shorts, found the kitchen knife, pulled it out, said, "Were you planning to peel potatoes or something?" and put it in his jacket pocket. Then, "Sit down and we'll talk."

The knife blade was still outward.

"Just to make things simpler," Al said, "I know who's upstairs and why she's upstairs."

For some reason this came as no surprise to Rob; he supposed that was why he had obeyed Al's commands so obediently, without an enraged defiant reaction of bone and muscle, no matter how reckless.

He pulled out a lyre-backed chair and sat down. Al chose the chair at right angles to him, appropriately enough at the head of the table.

"Okay," he said. Meeting being called to order, but unlike men in business meetings, Al did not clear his throat and tee off with a lavish waste of words. "How much?"

"How much what?"

"I said, how much?" He very lightly, with a grimace, drew his thumbnail across his throat. "After all, she's not my mother."

Rob swallowed. "Twenty-five thousand . . ."

The born gamber, Al said, "Not from what Mouse said. Shall I or shall I not go upstairs?"

Mouse. Like a hard whack between the shoulders, driving
he breath from his lungs. No, wrong; if Mouse had spelled it
ut why should he be asking *him?* A bluff, probably. Too dan-
erous right this minute to call his bluff.

"Times ten," Rob said, looking Al very directly in the eye.
More and more things didn't seem to matter any longer; ex-
ept one.

Al shaped his mouth for what might have been a whistle
ut forbore to produce it; the tense rounded lips gave his face
peculiar dark merriment. His astonishment and pleasure
vere obvious for one naked second before he relaxed his
nouth and smoothed his features again.

Rob looked over and above Al's shoulder at a painted dead
oose hanging upside down, with a dead rabbit lying cross-
vays, and a bunch of yellow grapes, and another of currants,
ach currant scrupulously painted, red as blood, bursting with
s own living inner juice.

"It's all very simple," Al said kindly, now a doctor to a nerv-
us patient. "I had a lot of time to think, while you and Mouse
vere screwing around with how fat the meat was, and where
vas the ketchup, and poor kitty, and blankets for cold nights,
nd milk and beer and things—"

In a remote distance, Rob saw him driving off in his white
onvertible, in the afternoon, and heard Mouse saying, "We
vere lucky we got rid of him . . . I don't even like to *think*
bout what could have happened . . ."

He forced himself back to his position of, for the moment,
bedient captive, and made himself listen.

". . . I'll join the party," Al was saying. "All for one and
ne for all. Three's company, in this case. For tomorrow, and
omorrow night."

He pushed a pack of cigarettes toward Rob. "Have one?"
"No thanks."

Al skillfully managed to light one with his free hand and
hen began to think out loud, studying Rob through smoke. It

helped that it all seemed quite unreal, Al generously lettin
him in on his thought processes.

"Well. What first of all are we going to do with you? I can
very well take your word of honor because last I heard there
no such thing. You're a big strong kid, we can't very well g
around night and day like Siamese twins, you and me and th
knife . . . and then sooner or later, Mouse will wake up . .
no point in asking you now where the money's to be put, yo
could tell me a wrong place and I could be barking up a tre
while maybe some buddy of yours or Mouse's could be pic
ing it up in the right place. I don't want to do anything to e
ther of you if I can help it, why complicate things, but . . .
guess no matter how you've treated her you want her set fre
and you've probably fixed it, told him, your old man, that tha
won't happen until the money's coughed up . . . so she's th
key to the whole thing, always was, of course. I can't ver
well say, You two kids go on home and play, I'll take care c
the business—though it would be simpler. One way or anothe
I'm stuck with you."

He took a last long pull at his cigarette, dropped it on th
carpet, and ground it out with the toe of his espadrille. Ro
said nothing.

His own mind had been, while recording every word A
said, racing along on its own lines. He can't very well kill me
or both of us, and maybe even—? Too much appalling troubl
for him ahead, two bodies, three— And he needs me alive t
show him where they'll put the stuff . . .

But Mouse knows, and yes, he could after all kill me. And i
he doesn't there are always ways to get someone to talk abou
something even if they swear at first to themselves they won't-
His mind backed away from this vision.

Concentrate on the end, the goal, not what happens alon
the road on the way to it. A long-ago semi-criticism on a re
port card from school came back to him from nowhere. "Rob
ert has leadership qualities which somewhat interfere with hi
cooperation and team spirit among his peers."

Shove leadership qualities, at least for now; he could by some big-deal who-cares plunge bring the roof down on all three of them.

"For the moment I guess the only thing is to file you away," Al mused. "Get up. Walk."

It was like a dream, the sense of repetition. Out into the kitchen, knife point at his back. "Stop at the sink and get yourself a big drink of water," Al said. "It may be a long time before the next one."

He never knew you could gag on water but he did, coughed, choked, and got a weird helping thump between the shoulder blades; then he got a full glass into him.

Down the cellar stairs, the same cellar stairs, along the familiar stony route—except that now there was a strange unpleasantly sweet stench that burned his nostrils a little.

"The place is full of rat poison," he said. "Or was."

"Tough shit," Al said, lovingly close behind him. "Let's hope and pray it's mostly—what's the word?—dissipated itself. Or maybe it doesn't hurt humans. You might try tying a handkerchief over your mouth and nose."

Straight ahead, into the wine cellar. No mattress, no blanket, no little comforts such as those provided for his mother.

"I'd like the light on."

People can go nuts, in the dark. They had left the light on for her.

"Okay." Al reached for the cord. He looked at Rob and started to back toward the door. "The knife not only works up close but I can throw it, I'm good at it," he warned as an uncontrollable threatening ripple ran over Rob's muscles.

The door was closed and the bolt shot home.

Rob stretched himself on the hard cool stone, face pillowed in his forearms. The reek wasn't so bad in here, maybe this part of the cellar had been done first, and it was well if mysteriously aired.

Then he let it happen. He burst into tears.

Mouse had experimented with various drugs and impatiently discarded them, like a child heaving toys out of it playpen. She took a strong daily dose of herself instead: essence of Mouse.

The sleeping pill hit her hard and she didn't wake until seven.

She opened her eyes to Al Madonna, sitting in Rob's big dark green chair, bent forward, watching her intently.

She immediately grasped what had happened, if not when and how it had happened. There wasn't a gasp from her, a slow take of any sort.

Raising herself on her elbow, she said, "And what have you done with Rob?"

"Stashed him away in the cellar, big room, lots of shelves—or racks?—nice bolt, and you wouldn't want a heavier door on a mausoleum. He's okay, I didn't touch him."

Time again for Miss Porter. "I gather we have a partner?"

"You gather damn right," Al said, grinning. His teeth were very white in his pocked red-brown face. "You pick up things fast, Mouse."

She saw the knife lying on the broad arm of the green chair a few inches away from his fingertips.

"You're not going to need that with me," she said calmly.

"No, I figured you'd work things out for yourself. You can't very well run away and shout help, because you can take it from me the police are on your tail. I could hurt him, or her or you, and I don't think you'd want that. No point in rocking the boat, there'll just be the difference of the three of us splitting, not two. Look at it this way—you're getting some professional help."

Mouse looked at it in quite another way. She couldn't imagine rapacious Al being meekly satisfied with his third of the money. Al was not a partner, not anyone's partner.

Al had, at least for now, taken over. She knew he had once killed a man; he had told her about it when he was a little drunk. "I felt funny—awful—for a day and a half . . ."

"And of course the biggest thing of all is I could call the police about you two. And run." Al thoughtfully fingered the dark stubble on his chin.

She threw off her sheet and put her bare feet to the floor and sat up on the sofa. "I'll play," she said.

"Good. I thought you would. You look nice for somebody who's just out of the sack. Don't bother trying to telephone anybody, the phone's fixed, nothing in, nothing out. And, oh yes, you don't have a gun anymore."

"Partners don't need guns and knives against each other," Mouse said sweetly. "I'm going upstairs to shower and change and I don't need a bodyguard while I'm doing it."

"No need for that, as I said you're pretty well boxed in. You won't mind if I wait *outside* the bathroom door?"

"Feel free." She picked up the tubular yellow beach bag she had tossed down long ago, yesterday, beside the velvet-skirted round table, and went up the stairs, lightly and softly followed by him. She took her time, a long steamy soapy shower, a leisurely scrubbing of teeth and brushing of hair, fresh underclothes, fresh jeans, a defiantly gay orange shirt.

Emerging, shining with rest and cleanliness and with what she recognized as a sharp stinging excitement, she said, "Yay, team! Come and help with the drill. Breakfast for Mrs. Defore. We do it in twos and now you're the other half."

"Breakfast for us first, I'm starving."

"You poor hungry crook," Mouse said over her shoulder, running down the stairs. In the kitchen, she got out a pound of bacon and a box of eggs.

"I like mine over," Al ordered, "and in the bacon fat, not butter. . . . It's cozy in here."

The rain had begun sometime in the night, heavy disorderly June rain dashing itself at the windowpanes. It was very dark outside the warm bright kitchen. Echoes of rain came down the back stairs and through the butler's pantry.

He went over to her as she was turning the bacon with a fork and kissed the back of her neck, where the heavy hair

split and slid on either side of the nape. His hand rested on
her shoulder. She moved her head a little and saw his nails
short and dirty.

". . . and I like my bacon well-done."

"Two eggs for you, two for me, two for Rob—I don't sup
pose you're planning to starve him?"

"No, he can eat, if he isn't rat-poisoned." Al threw back his
head and laughed. He was close against her and she could
feel his taut excitement, meeting hers. A crazy chancy game to
play, the winner not determined yet.

"God yes, I forgot the exterminator boy— And not fried but
boiled, for Mrs. Devore, will you see to the toast?"

She thumped on the table a loaf of what she called ooey
gooey bread, white, soft, thick, sliced; she had been brought
up on homemade bread baked by the Astons' German cook.

Al wasn't used to being ordered by females to undertake
cooking tasks, but he manned the toaster as one trying a nov
elty, snatched out the slices when they popped up, and but
tered them heavily and unevenly.

"Is she all right?" he asked, buttering. "I heard her talking
to herself last night." In a superstitious way, he didn't want to
say that he had heard her at her prayers.

"She's okay. Pour out a glass of orange juice for her, please,
and the coffee's ready, if you want a cup before I finish. Why
won't eggs and bacon ever come out at the same time?"

They consumed their breakfasts in hungry silence.

Then, "Ladies first, I suppose?" Al said.

"Yes, if you'll hand me the tray—"

A three-minute boiled egg, two slices of toast, the orange
juice, a cup of coffee. ("Ma likes one teaspoon of sugar and a
very light dash of milk.")

"No point in making things worse by having her worry
about something having happened to Rob," Mouse said
thoughtfully. "You stand outside the door when I go in, I'll
call you Rob from inside the room, don't say anything. Of
course if she— Of course you'll have to be ready, just in case."

"Okay, I'd just as soon she didn't see me."

Mouse's hand, reaching for the salt and pepper, halted in midair.

"Why?"

"You've got a lot to learn about this game," Al said, adding patiently, "If she doesn't see me, she'll be all right, if you know what I mean."

19

Properly looked at, Madeline told herself, it was all but over
One more day, and a portion of a night. What was one day!

On Morton Street, it was no sooner Monday morning than i
was the next Friday evening, the weekend delightfully ahead
Devore allowed himself to be moderately lazy on weekends
they would drive to the house in Greens Farms if they felt like
it, or salvage some of the pleasures of a great city grown in
creasingly frightening. Stroll through the Metropolitan, th
Museum of Modern Art. Take tremendous long window
browsing walks down Third Avenue, or Madison, or Fifth
Stop for drinks and lunch at any one of a string of favorit
restaurants. They had once liked wandering through the dra
matic empty silences of Wall Street on Sundays, it was fas
cinating being the only living creatures for blocks and blocks
but that had to be given up, it wasn't great fun to be absc
lutely alone in New York anymore.

Whenever they happened to walk by Devore House she al
ways blessed herself; this never failed to amuse him. "What
that for?" he had asked the first time. Laughing, leaning close
against his side for a moment, "For being given you, c
course." She forgot to do it just once and he had said severel
"Am I to assume you've taken a lover?"

Yes, the weekend was, really, right around the corner. How marvelous. How remote.

Rain hit the window hard on a gust of wind. It was dark outside, very dark for eight o'clock in the morning. A branch of weeping spruce dipped and shuddered outside the one clear window. She had read until midnight and then taken two of Rob's aspirins and slept in insecure snatches, body wanting rest, mind relentlessly on guard. One of them would be asleep but one of them would be awake, somewhere, downstairs.

One of them, thinking: It's too dangerous—do I want *that* hanging over my head all my life? No matter how you look at it, the simplest thing is to—

Not Rob, though. Not Rob?

In a seized desperation of calm, she did her hair and made the bed and picked up her bell and rang it.

A minute or two later, there was a ludicrously polite knock, the door was unbolted, and Mouse came in and put the tray down on the bedside table. No gun this time? Then she saw the handles of the long scissors thrust into the back pocket of Mouse's jeans.

"Bathroom or breakfast first?" Mouse inquired.

Madeline sensed some change in her, the cool flat manner elevated to some pitch of expectancy, excitement. The change terrified her.

"Breakfast," she said. Must pull her voice down, it was too high. "And alone, if I may."

Mouse raised her own voice a little. "Everything's okay, Rob, you can go on down, I'll wait outside and then do shower duty, and I think I left the heat on under the coffee-pot, will you turn it off?"

Rob: ". . . you won't be drugged, this stuff is safe, and you really have to eat . . ."

People didn't have to, after all, be drugged to be disposed of in a final fashion. She made herself drink the orange juice and coffee and eat the egg but left the limp butter-drenched toast.

Then—odd how the little humiliations could temporarily overshadow the basic freezing fears—she rang her bell again to be allowed to go down to the bathroom.

"Nasty day," Mouse said conversationally behind her as they went down the stairs.

What, oh God, what was that strange dark shine on her?

"I'll be right outside," Mouse said. "I've got these." She patted her back pocket.

"Yes. I saw."

Mouse leaned against the bathroom door and looked at Al sitting six steps down, watching her. Suddenly, catching himself by surprise, he sneezed.

Through her tooth-brushing noises, Madeline heard the sneeze—peculiarly touching, human sound—and thought simultaneously: He's caught a cold, and, That isn't Rob's sort of sneeze. She had to remind herself, putting the toothbrush back in the rack, that this was no time to let her mind start slipping. Splitting hairs, examining the tune and texture of spasmodic and violent expiration of breath.

Any fool could keep a mind reined in, a body obedient to it, for just one day, one last day.

Mouse had kept Rob's plate of bacon and eggs warm on top of a gently steaming pot of water, under a pot lid.

"Fancy catering around here," Al said, fingertips touching the gun in his pocket. "All ready?"

"Yes. You go first, light the lights as you go—"

"You go first," Al said.

Musical chairs, Mouse said to herself, back for a moment in a buried time, smocked white dimity dress just above her round knees, expensive party, she must have been eight or nine. A magician there, and someone to play the piano, everything organized, delicious food, mothers busy on martinis and producing little waves of laughter from the living room. N

matter when the music stopped she always had her bottom
firmly on a chair, no matter who had to be pushed aside or
unseated. Wails, "That's not *fair*," from some child on the
floor.

Me in front and *he* in back of me with the gun. Enjoy yourself, Al. While it lasts.

Al had suddenly, and without any social qualifications,
joined Them. Authority, rules, domination—take-over people
he had long since discarded.

Moving in and spoiling things.

Rob had slept a little, on and off, and thought very hard,
and found he kept thinking himself into dead ends. *She* hadn't
had a prayer of getting out of here. Neither did he, unless—

He took a long sniff at the air. The reek was almost gone;
here was just a sweet sinister memory of it left.

Earlier, he had investigated the wine casks. Too heavy, too
awkwardly shaped to be thrown with any speed or accuracy.
He could be caught in mid-hurl. A thrown knife, a bullet, and
he wouldn't be any good to her wounded, or worse—

Then this was the only thin chance.

At four-forty by his watch, he put his forefinger down his
throat and made himself vomit copiously on the stone floor.
There might be a little left, he could try again later.

Remembering an old trick of his school days, when he
wanted for some reason to stay home, he went to the wine
shelves, rubbed the tips of his fingers in dust, and applied the
dust under his eyes, stroking it in well. Hard, without a mirror; too little would be more convincing than too much. At
home he had used cigarette ash, but none was at present
available. It always worked. (Ma, coming in to wake him, a
slow opening of his eyes and a long sigh; sometimes he used a
little of her bath powder too, white, rubbed in over cheeks
and forehead. "I feel funny, Ma, sick, sort of . . ." "You *look*
sick, your eyes . . . Just stay in bed, try to sleep some more,

I'll look in in an hour or so . . ." Temperature taken, no tem
perature. "It's my stomach that feels funny . . .")

He lay down and watched the hours go by. At around
seven, shuddering and retching, he managed to produce an
other small pool.

It was the hardest effort of his life to keep his eyes closed
when there was the sound of the bolt being pulled back and
they came in.

A half gasp, half shriek escaped Mouse. "My God, is he
dead . . . ? The rat poison, oh God . . . look, he's been sick
all over the place . . ."

Hand invadingly on his shirt, over his heart, not Mouse's
hand, Al's.

"Ticking away. What if he's faking it?"

"With all this vomit? . . . And look at his eyes, look at that
horrible color under them, I've never seen him like this."

Rob stirred and uttered a very faint sighing groan. He kept
his eyes closed.

"We can't leave him here, we can't let him die . . ."

"What do you think you're going to do about him? Call a
doctor?"

"Don't be crazy . . . but they use stomach pumps and
things for poison, don't they? And he's emptied his stomach
already. . . . Look, he's *shivering* . . ."

The shiver had been spontaneous, induced by the voices
above his head, the not knowing whose side Mouse was on,
the fear that at any moment he might be kicked in the head
by Al, or in the guts, to see if his frightening illness was real—

"We can't leave him here on this cold floor. We'll have to
get him to bed right away, warm—"

"*Hell*, Mouse." Strong resistance in Al's voice. "Let him
pull himself together down here."

"If you want to be practical, it would be dangerous if he
died," Mouse said. "Bodies and things. He couldn't be left
here because after tomorrow, I mean after today, this house
will be shown by the real estate people. And it would be—

suppose, leaving him here to pass out for good—murder—manslaughter?"

Mutinous silence.

"And what could a flat-out sick kid do to you anyway? You're armed, at least with that knife."

"At least," Al said. At this prod to his vanity, he gave in. "Oh Christ, all right, I'll take his head and shoulders, you take his feet."

They managed the deliberately limp weight, slowly, clumsily, up the cellar stairs, Al swearing under his breath at the effort. Their patient's head struck hard against a doorjamb and he groaned again.

"Couch?" Al asked hopefully.

"No, a bedroom, he has to have quiet. Look at him, all gray and ghastly . . ."

Up the stairs from the hall, where the stained-glass windows had gone numb from the lack of light, stony purple and dull liver-red.

"The last bedroom on the right," Mouse directed, panting.

"Why?" he asked suspiciously.

"Why? It's right next to the back staircase down to the kitchen, we'll be in there a lot, we can hear him from there."

They put him, clothed, between white sheets. At Al's end it was more a dumping than a laying down of their burden.

"I wish he'd open his eyes," Mouse said. She placed a tentative palm, which had no idea what it was feeling for, on his forehead.

"He's cold. Or damp. And hot too."

"Leave him be, I'm sick of him," Al said. He looked thoughtfully at the three big windows. "I guess in the shape he's in he won't try to climb out. Let's see, are they noisy?" He unlocked one and raised the lower sash; it made a loud complaining sound of wood against wood. A waterfall swishing sound of rain poured into the room.

"Anyway," Al added, very slowly and clearly, "if he tried to cut and run, I'd be off like a shot to the telephone and let the police take over. I'm clean. Just a voice, just someone who stumbled onto a real rotten trick."

He beckoned to Mouse. "Come on, nursie, I'm not leaving you alone with him."

Outside the door, he reached for one of two straight chairs flanking a lamp table. He was about to wedge it under the knob when Mouse said, "No, don't—suppose he has to throw up again, or go to the bathroom?"

As he hesitated, with the chair in his hand, she laughed a little. "You're not afraid of him, are you, Al?"

He put the chair back against the wall. Still speaking carefully, voice raised, he said to the door, "Now that you put it that way, he has two, no, three good reasons to be afraid of me."

20

During the night, Devore and Titus spelled each other, one of them in theory to take his turn to sleep.

Titus said didactically, "It's a medically proven fact that if you lie still in the dark, and compose yourself, and don't thrash around, your body gets eighty-eight percent of the rest it gets when you're actually asleep."

On Thursday morning he took most of the telephone calls. Calls from a normal world left behind. A dinner party next Tuesday. Pat Guedella: "Will you tell Madeline I did pick up the canapé? I got it for two hundred, and there's only one place on the cane that needs repairing." Did Mrs. Devore want her furs stored? Disbrow's Meat Market: "Mrs. D. asked us to let her know when the Dover sole came in."

Mrs. Boland called a little before noon and asked in an anxiously casual way for Madeline. "Not here at the moment," Titus said. "I dropped around to return a book. . . . Hugh's here, but he's in the shower."

In the shower at this ungodly hour? Why wasn't he at work?

"Well, Jane, then."

Mrs. Boland was worried about Jane, and through her sensed something badly wrong in the Devore household. She was also consumed with curiosity about Madeline's absence, or silence, or both. Perhaps a terrible hidden long-brewing crisis suddenly exploding, Madeline leaving, maybe Devore had taken up with another woman . . . After all, he was *very* attractive, a kind of electric, radiating male. But they had seemed such an almost oddly loving, *happy*—but then it happened all the time.

Jane was sitting on the living-room floor. Returning, as she had done a dozen times during her waking hours, to a litter of road maps.

The evening before, in one of his frequent memory-scourings, Titus said, "Well, back to New Jersey." He thought it highly likely that that was where she was; why further complicate a desperate deed by spreading it over two states?

He had recited, "New Brunswick? Morristown, South River, Plainfield, Ringoes, Lambertville, Phillipsburg, Hopewell?" (Of ghastly memories, but Jane wouldn't know about Hopewell, and the Lindbergh baby.) "Collingswood, Toms River, Cape May, Montclair, Bloomfield, Tenafly, Lakehurst, Avalon, Stone Harbor?"

"No . . ." Jane said, her face a mask of trouble.

Devore said, his voice tight, "I think you'll drive all of us crazy, Walter. There may be after all nothing in it and you may be just clamming up her mind one way or another—"

Nothing in it or perhaps everything, locked behind Jane's broad silky forehead.

Patiently, Titus said, "Things heard have a different cadence than things read, on a map or anywhere."

Cadence. Jane, for some reason fascinated by the word, said it over in her mind.

In her distress, she went down a little side alley. "I never realized before what funny names people give towns. Peapack, Pluckemin, Succasunna, Tranquility, Glen Gardner . . . and here's a Titusville . . ."

A long furious sigh from her father shut her up.

It was all he could do not to take her by the shoulders and

savagely try to shake the name out of her, the town, the place where Madeline might be. If—round and round—there was anything in it at all.

Jane felt his raging impatience and his bleak disappointment in her. The thing that maddened her was, had she heard the name at all, and would she recognize it if she saw it? But then, if she hadn't heard it, why had she been reminded of thrift, and virtue?

"Rachel Boland for you," Titus said, summoning Jane from her renewed quest on the floor. "Mind what you say."

Jane gave him a glance of elderly scorn.

"Jane, dear, we're driving up to Old Lyme a bit later," Mrs. Boland said, "to collect Prue from my sister's. The train service from there is almost nonexistent, buses and taxis and all kinds of things to make connections. Would you like to come with us? It's a pretty drive even in the rain."

Prue was Elizabeth's nine-year-old sister. Prue Boland. Prudence Anne Boland.

She had seen the name on the map—when, an hour ago?— and felt a jump of excitement. But then she thought, Elizabeth, New Jersey, and Prudence, New Jersey, the two Bolands . . . maybe she was going a little crazy, or like her mother said, round the bend.

Things heard have a different cadence than things read—
Cadence. Prue. Prudence.

Jane made a peculiar sound and dropped the receiver to the rug. Titus, with a look at her face, picked it up and said, "Someone at the door, Rachel, she'll call you right back."

Jane was already running up the stairs. *"Daddy—"* voice close to a scream.

The bathroom door shot open and Devore stood in it, dripping and towel-wrapped, unable to move for a second or speak. His mind had stopped in its tracks at her cry, or turned itself off as the mind does when staring final disaster in the face.

"I think I know where she is," Jane said, panting. "If it *is* Mouse's aunt's house where they— It's in Prudence, New Jersey."

"No, of course you can't go with us," Devore said. "I want you to go to Old Lyme with Rachel, I don't want you here alone—come on, Jane, you've been marvelous so far."

It was probably a mirage in the desert, this beckoning town; there would be no lifesaving shade and water in it at all. But it was in any case action, occupation, to allow the body for a while to take over from the awfulness inside the head.

"All right," Jane said. She had gone very pale, pale as he was, but now a rosiness returned to her face. Maybe she had done something, maybe she had really helped. They would just plain go and get her mother and just plain bring her home. Rob wouldn't be able to stand up to her father face to face, she was pretty sure of that.

There was a wait while the Copeland Banking and Trust Company prepared to meet its new delivery schedule. More than an hour later Malcolm Copeland called Devore back.

"Don't like to have all that cash sending out radar signals to interested people. As you hadn't made your police arrangements clear, we have a young man—excuse the scruff—repairing his motorcycle across the street from your garage. Your keys are inside the green watering can just to the right of the doors. Good luck, Hugh."

Titus found something to be thankful for in the violence of the rain.

"At least they won't be sunbathing on that high hill of theirs that commands all approach roads, didn't he say? I assume you've got some kind of plan, Hugh."

Devore, at the wheel of his Mercedes, intent on the road, said, "Something like this. Walk up to the door, knock, or ring. Here's the money, hand over your mother, and off you go. And that will be that."

"What will be what?" Titus looked sideways at him and went on carefully, "You don't think that if and when we track down the house you might then back yourself up with police? Invisible of course?"

"No. If I don't believe I'm absolutely on the level, they won't believe it either. These things show. I've never said anything to him I didn't mean, and he knows it."

". . . and off you go," Titus repeated.

"It's Madeline I want, and I don't give a damn what happens after that." The sudden agonized deepening of a crease on his long cheek belied that. "I'll give them a couple of hours' lead time, I'll promise them that, before I call in the constabulary. As you said, they're good at dropping out, but that's their problem. Just a few minutes to buy, and sell, and bargain, it ought to be reasonably simple."

At the scald in his voice, Titus made his own voice deliberately everyday, casual. "Just walk up and knock on the door," he said, and answered himself. "Yes, why not? It's highly unlikely that he and the girl, or whoever his pal is, would land themselves with two large male corpses. And they must have figured it out that by now the police are on their tail."

He had been in touch with the police and the FBI during the night and the morning. They were working hard and were just a degree or so past nowhere.

The "Ashton" girl's name turned out to be Aston and Connecticut telephone directories had been combed. A call at eleven-ten, one of thirty Aston calls, aroused, in Greenwich, a maid with a tired-sounding black voice. Mr. and Mrs. Aston had gone to see friends off for Kenya at Kennedy International Airport and said that as it would be late they would stay with other friends "somewhere on Long Island" and be back sometime tomorrow. Yes, there was a daughter, yes, she was called Mouse. The Astons didn't know where she lived and neither did the maid. They used a box number to send her checks. Did the Astons have a city apartment or another country place, beach house, something like that? No, sir, only this residence, they stay at the St. Regis when they're in New York.

A boy at the Clipjoint said he and Rob and some other friends had shared a house the summer before at Water Island on Fire Island. It could be empty; the season didn't peak on Fire Island until after the Fourth of July. A police helicopter flew out; the house had burned down at some time during the winter and sat black and ruined in the rain.

Other slender leads were fruitlessly followed, in Princeton, New Jersey; North Conway, Vermont; Newburgh, New York.

No trace, no whisper of Mrs. Devore and her son and his friend or friends.

"She's got to be somewhere," Titus said, to break the bleak rain-rushing silence and cheer himself. "And this could be it. Good timing, I *think*—not anywhere near the crisis hours."

In spite of the downpour, rain sizzling a foot high off the cement and ramming from the east at the car windows, traffic on the Garden State was heavy and looked in places like a convention of buses. Titus glanced at his map and said, "The next exit after this one."

He had telephoned ahead to make a roughish appointment at what he found to be the one real estate office in Prudence, Cove and Sniffen. His appointment was with a Mr. Cove. "Sometime between two forty-five or three-fifteen or so, depending on traffic, I want to be sure you'll be there, I'm driving from New York and the rain might tie things up."

"I'll be here," Mr. Cove assured him. Business couldn't be any slower; it had been three weeks since he'd moved anything, and that was just five acres of the Rigby estate, part of it undesirable swamp, that old Clara Rigby wanted to dispose of.

The caller from New York hadn't stated his business. But, thought Mr. Cove, what do you come to a real estate office for but to deal in real estate one way or another, to buy or sell, keep the ball rolling? He also dealt in insurance, but he could think of no reason why someone should drive here from New York to take out an insurance policy with his firm. Too bad about the weather, even the best places didn't shine out in the rain.

His office was above a cheese-and-wine shop a little off the village green. As this was Prudence, the two commercial enterprises occupied a very old prim white clapboard house abutting on the sidewalk with window boxes full of battered drenched pansies.

They went up the stairs. On an open combination landing-office at the top, they identified themselves to what was evidently the girl-of-all-work and she waved them through the open door to her right. "You're expected."

There was a center space with an oblong table and chairs, and an enclosed office to the right and to the left. Mr. Cove was discovered at his desk attempting to look prosperously busy, going rapidly through papers in a stack of manila folders. He rose to greet them as they went in, Devore very firmly closing the door behind him and leaning against it; his legs felt odd.

Titus said, "Sit down, Mr. Cove," bent toward him and murmured, "Maximum security matter. CIA."

He produced no credentials and Mr. Cove asked for none. He got an impression of unmistakable authority from the mild murmur, the pince-nez, the heron stoop.

"We want a list of houses, estates, in and around Prudence, which are for rent or for sale, or which are for the time being unoccupied, owners away somewhere, you'd know about that."

God bless me, Mr. Cove thought, what an exciting thing to happen on a rainy day. Was the other man CIA too, the dark-haired silent one?

He got out a card file so as to look crisply efficient to this agent, or whatever he was called, although he knew by heart all the places asked for.

"Let me see," forefinger flicking busily. "There's a carriage house for rent on the Curriers' estate . . ." and responding to his salesman's instincts like a knee to the hammer, said, ". . . the Curriers would allow the tenants to share the pool, an Olympic-sized one—"

"We don't want a house, Mr. Cove, we just want to look them over," Titus said patiently.

"Yes, of course, and they're there, anyway, at the big house. Mmmmm . . . Garner estate, two hundred seventy-five thousand dollars, suitable for a riding academy—" and he added hastily, entering into the spirit of the thing, "I only mention that because there are extensive outbuildings, stables—"

He was bursting with curiosity. Did the CIA try to catch people over back taxes? Some of these millionaires around here— Well, no, hardly.

As he vocally listed properties, he obligingly scribbled street names and numbers on a pad. Wyndham house, one wing burned, fifty acres, greenhouses intact. The Luries' place, the Alastair Luries'—they were in Russia. Mrs. Malone had been taken to the hospital from her house, but her butler and cook were in residence. Then there was the Aston place.

"The Aston place?" Titus adjusted his pince-nez.

Mr. Cove had been feeling a little guilty, unprofessional, about that pair. But after all there'd been a nibble, a thin chance at a sale. He fumbled it out. "—There's a young couple staying there for a few days, a little . . . unusual in a house for sale, which of course should be ready to be shown at any and all hours."

The man against the door made a peculiar sound in his throat.

Mr. Cove gave him a startled look and resumed his explanations. "But she's the niece, showed me correct identification—if it wasn't, now that I think of it, borrowed—Margaret Aston. Not drifters, you know, perfectly clean and respectable-looking young people as these things go today— And the house, not being sold, is technically still in the family's hands, although Grace Aston's brother is the heir. The girl said his, the boy's, family might consider buying the place and they'd let me know one way or another by tomorrow. Wanted to be left by themselves for I don't like to think what."

Mr. Cove took off his glasses and polished them. "So I thought—"

"Thank you, Mr. Cove, most helpful. We'll want the keys to the Garner, Wyndham, and Aston places," Titus demanded politely. "And you'd be well-advised to keep our conference entirely to yourself."

Mr. Cove, who had read in the newspapers a great deal about CIA matters and methods ("And at that," he had said gloomily last month to his wife, "top of the iceberg"), agreed without reservations.

21

"Just in case he conks out for good, I suppose you know where the money'll be put? Not that I think . . . but it never hurts, covering bases."

They were in the kitchen. Mouse was making sandwiches for them, cheese and baloney.

"We're all but out of food, good thing there's only one more day to get through—"

She was sorely tempted to say she didn't know but then he might go up and go after Rob, maybe hurt him, to make him tell.

For both of them, she had to keep up a show of jauntiness, confidence. She knew instinctively that Al admired her nerve and guts and might deal with her more pleasantly than he would with a trembling, placating victim; that would bring out the worst in him.

"Of course I know, but if you think I'm going to draw a map for you at the moment, you're crazy. That would leave you completely in charge, wouldn't it?"

"In case you don't know it, I *am* completely in charge. Or let's say senior partner if you like that better. I don't want any mustard on mine, but plenty of butter." He grinned at her. "It doesn't matter where anyway, I mean, I'll just stick to your side like a burr when we go collecting."

She put his sandwich in front of him without comment.

"And don't, any time, try to get smart and jump me. If you do I'll really put your playmate out of business. Glass of wine, please."

"There's only enough for Mrs. Devore's cocktail time."

"Screw Mrs. Devore's cocktail time. I'm thirsty."

"I think I'd better make Rob some tea," Mouse said. From the sick-stomach days of early childhood she remembered the cups of hot sweet milky tea. "And some toast."

She had gone up to see him several times during the morning, Al close on her heels. She wasn't sure that by now he wasn't faking it; a clear fresh color had come into his cheeks, but there was still the dark stain under his eyes. He lay with his face to the wall, breathing evenly.

His bedcovers were kicked and lashed around, though. God, he hadn't had *convulsions?* Dying people, she had read somewhere, often wore an expression of peace. But on closer examination his face didn't look peaceful at all, the mouth hard, the corners of it turned downward, an unfamiliar crease between the butterscotch-colored eyebrows.

They ate their sandwiches and she prepared the invalid food. Outside Rob's door, she said, "Let me go in alone with this, I'll have to wake him up, there might be fighting, trouble, you might lose your temper—like you said, why rock the boat?"

Al had his hand in his demin jacket pocket. She had long since recorded the shape of the bulge in it. "Okay. Leave the door open some."

She went over to the bed and put a hand on Rob's shoulder. He rolled over on his back instantly, eyes wide open, brilliantly clear. She put the back of her hand to her forehead and made a face, which he read easily to mean that he still felt awful.

He groaned faintly. His arms were outside the sheet; she saw his hands slowly clench and felt from him the held-in power of a crouching, waiting tiger.

As though passing along the weather report, she said, "Al's outside. He has his gun and ours seems to be missing. . . . Try to get this tea down, Rob, and at least a slice of toast. And I've got to do something about your bed, it's all torn to pieces."

"I don't think I can . . ." Obediently draggy, petulant voice, not at the moment interested in guardians with guns.

"Well, try. Here, sit up, I'll fix your pillows."

Straightening the sheet, tucking it in, pulling the blanket up, she hummed to herself, and then began to sing rapidly in a startlingly sweet soft voice. She sang in French.

One of Rob's majors before he left college, she knew, was languages; he was good at them.

To the tune of "Frère Jacques," Mouse sang, "Just stay there, just stay there, be horribly sick and wretched, I'll try to work something out, see if you can throw up your tea and toast after you get it down, we've got to manage him somehow or other."

Song turning into humming again, she left the room.

"What the hell are you singing about?" Al asked. "Some kid's song, I forget the name—"

"I always sing when I'm excited," Mouse said, her cheeks flaring pink, her eyes invitingly raking him from head to toe and back again. "Too bad we can't both be off duty at once, Al. But one thing at a time. Let's wait here a bit to see if it stays down, I'm kind of worried about him, he looks terrible. Oh God—"

There were desperate retching sounds from the bedroom.

"You clean it up," Mouse said. "After all, it's your problem too. You put him down there, with the poison."

"Are you kidding? I have to have the use of both hands, with you two. You three. Kitchen now, an errand."

"Yes, Mrs. Devore's lunch, it's late already—"

"She can't very well clear out of this restaurant if she doesn't like the service she's getting."

In the kitchen, Al investigated drawers and pulled out a pair of thin plastic gloves. Under the sink, he found a cham-

bis. "Give me your hand, Mouse, you're going to take a little
walk with me." His grip was a hard no-nonsense one.

Close beside him, she watched as, gloves on, he circled the
kitchen, rubbing busily with his chamois. Doorknobs, counter
surfaces, the wall phone he said he'd fixed, the doorjamb, the
drawer handles. "I'll superintend your washing up, that'll take
care of glasses and knives and forks and things."

Fingerprints. *They* had been going to drop out afterward,
but Al Madonna wasn't. He was just going to go merrily
along, playing himself. As far as a police check was con-
cerned, he would never have been there, in that house. Just a
wild story she and Rob had thought up.

There was something scary about it, something terribly real
and businesslike. In a voice that didn't sound to her quite
right, she asked, "How many times have you been arrested?"

"Just once, fifteen, stolen car. They never even sniffed me
on the bigger stuff," Al boasted.

The eerie housekeeping, the conscientious rubbing and pol-
ishing, was continued in the dining room, the hall, the porch;
on the stairway banister, in the bathroom, on the back of
the chair opposite Rob's slightly open door. "They might
be able to pick up something from his clothes, where we
carried him—we'll burn those later."

Rob, his throat raw and his stomach muscles still sore with
the effort of throwing up, staying still, heard this as he lay on
his back and stared at the ceiling.

We've got to manage him somehow or other—

He himself was, for the moment, stuck with the role of poor
puking Rob. Get up on two feet, show himself able to walk
and he'd be back in the cellar. Have to, Christ, just lie here
until Mouse came up with her somehow-or-other.

He had been thinking the same things she was probably
thinking, back and forth, round and round, his head ringing
with it.

At first, the only centrally important thing had been to get

out of the wine cellar, within emergency helping distance o
his mother. If there was any—his mind supplied the only eu
phemism bearable now—trouble. Of any kind.

What if I were Al? he thought. A professional crook, a one
man gang, stumbling by luck into this. A quarter of a millior
dollars.

Now, if I were Al (be calm, be cold, be objective) I woul
naturally want all the money for myself.

Particularly as they don't know about me, Al, those peopl
who are looking for Rob Devore and his girl. Al is a cipher, a
zero, Al doesn't to the authorities exist.

What would be the smartest, cleanest thing for him to do
Take all the money and hand *them* in, the known kidnappers
hand them in by telephone if you were lucky—

Police lights blazing in his eyes. Interrogation. "But i
wasn't us, I mean, it was us at first, but then he came in an
took over—"

Hardly a statement to pull at police heartstrings.

And unless in any encounter with Ma he was masked, uni
dentifiable, the cleanest, smartest thing to do about he
was . . .

The arrangements, a voice gabbled in his mind in hasty re
treat. Would Mouse pass them on to Al or would she kee
them to herself? In either case Al needn't even enter th
scene, just follow behind them and order a transfer of money

The arrangements . . . he, Rob, had originally been goin
to face up to telling her this evening, when they brought he
dinner tray.

Nothing to worry about, Ma, it's all but over. We'll leav
the house during the night. We need a little time to—well, yo
know. We'll unbolt your bedroom door when we go. In cas
you want to take a bath or something. There'll be a man,
friend of ours, downstairs, so I'd more or less stay up here if
were you but I don't think he'u hurt you." (An invented mar
but he ought to serve the purpose, he couldn't see his mothe
tiptoeing down the stairs to an unknown violence now th

he'd gotten through safely so far.) "He'll stay in the house till
even and then he'll leave. We've called a cab that's to come
out from town and pick you up at eight o'clock and take you
o the bus station. Here's twenty-five dollars, plenty to get you
o New York, and here's change, you might want to call home
before you get on the bus . . .

Goodbye, Ma.

Leave out that he'd been trying to stop it, when he met Al
coming down the stairs, with his knife.

Leave it out because he had started it, all of his own, and
Mouse's, free will, started something that couldn't be stopped.

For Madeline, time in its strange new way lurched ahead,
or went sideways, or ceased altogether. A moment being a
kind of forever, and then an hour slithering by, lost, leaving
no tracks behind it. She slept, on and off, more than she
thought was healthy, or even safe—the sleeper come upon
defenseless and unaware. She wasn't even sure, though, that it
could properly be called sleep: a blankness, eyes closed, a
moving into silence, certainly some kind of unconsciousness.

Now for the thirtieth time, she told herself—waiting for
something to eat and wondering how she could possibly be
wanting it—nothing at all may happen to me. It's just like
COD in reverse.

. . . But if something was going to be planned to happen,
this final day, it didn't do at all to sit cravenly waiting for it,
neck on the block. Hope and prayer were in their way helpful,
even unavoidable; but another kind of prayer can be your
own body and mind in action, working for survival.

There must be something in this bare little room that would
serve as a weapon to defend herself with. Defend herself
against a gun? A thrown object could conceivably knock a
gun from a hand.

("Your aim is terrible," Hugh said to her from the deep
past, when she was trying to toss a ball through a far doorway
in the apartment for their wedding-present toy poodle. "Don't

the Sisters of the Sacred Heart teach a young girl *anything?*"

The leather-cased clock was small and would require pin pointed aim. A sandal wasn't heavy enough. The thermos bot tle of cold water was awkward, she couldn't even get he hand around it properly.

She had only given, sometime long ago, a cursory inspectio to the small closet. She had no need for it; her clothes wer folded in the open suitcase on the floor. On the way to th closet she passed a little oval mirror. It showed her a pale lo face against a dark rushing backdrop of rain, hair neat, caugh up in its chignon, stranger's eyes looking back at her. Th woman, Robert Devore's mother, Hugh Devore's wife, fo marrying whom he was going to have to pay heavily, one wa or another.

The closet bar held a few wire hangers and an ancien sexless dark wool robe. There was a semi-ovaled white shap toward the back of the high shelf; she stood up on tiptoe an reached for it and as she did was suddenly back in the dinin room on Morton Street. Gay even in the rain, with Hugh green floors that always looked in any light like fresh sunl grass, and Boston fern and caladium and lavender lantan patterning the windowpanes.

The plastic hanging basket, which had probably once hun in the clear window, was mysteriously and miraculously fu of old, grayed dirt. It swung by its three nylon cords from he fingers, handleable, dangerous. It could be slung underhan and showers of dirt might help.

She took this precious object and pushed it just under th bed at the end nearest the door, moved her chair close to i and sat down.

If only, bringing her lunch, Mouse would come in alone.

Of course, that had been Rob's sneeze; of course, there wa no one in the house but the three of them. If she could g past Mouse, get to Rob—

She knew he was weakening. She had watched the erosic of his participation in this deadly game, and thought that th gun-carrying girl had probably taken over, providing spine and staying power for both of them. That airy explanation she had given of the sound of the shot crashing through the house, ". . . Rob and I had a little difference of opinion . . . you know how, in old movies, westerns, they fire at a glass of whiskey, to show how good their aim is . . ."

Secure Mouse in this room, as they had, so many times, secured her. Run and find a Rob who had existed, lived and breathed for nineteen years and three months, until the other was born on Tuesday night.

Save her own possibly threatened life and in a way perhaps his. "If we stop it now, we can consider it never happened, don't you agree?"

It wouldn't be true, there would be disfiguring scars, but they would be scars on flesh-and-blood creatures.

There was the sound of the bolt being jerked back. Bringing her lunch, Mouse came in alone.

22

In a thought-out sequence of motion, learned in these few minutes by heart and by hand, Madeline while rising from her chair flung the hanging basket at Mouse, advancing.

It struck her hard, on the left shoulder. The tray flew into the air, Mouse staggered sideways and fell, and began screaming amid the breaking and tinkling sounds and the thud of the basket against the wall, showering dirt.

Madeline had her hand on the doorknob when Al Madonna flung himself through the doorway. "Jesus Christ, Mouse, what—"

They stood face to face, inches from each other. She saw first an appalled look in his eyes, as though he had been tricked into some kind of terrible, final mistake. And then he gave his head a sharp shake and went to pull Mouse to her feet.

"*Ma!*" A frantic running shout from the stairway, and Rob was in the room.

"Bitch, bitch, bitch!" Mouse shrieked. "She's maybe broken my collarbone—"

Rob went over to Madeline and put his body between hers and Mouse's. Turning his head, he asked anxiously, "Are you all right, Ma?"

She had great difficulty in getting the words out. They echoed in her own ears from a far place. "I didn't know there were three of you, but I should have. The sneeze. It was like confusing a robin with a blue jay."

Al wondered if her imprisonment had sent her slightly nutty. She looked ten years older than she had looked when he faced her at the door. She sounded like a woman who had gone away somewhere else . . . Crazy. Back to business. He caught Mouse's hand as she bent swooping for the tray, evidently in her rage about to hurl it at her attacker.

With the other hand, he took out his gun. He let go of Mouse and backed to the door, the immediate danger of him, the deadliness, announced on air fallen silent.

Rob made himself half sit, half fall on the bed in a humbling, invalid sprawl.

"Well, convenient in a way, this get-together," Al was saying. "Gives me a little breathing time." He eased himself out and firmly shot the bolt.

Madeline stood looking at the remains of her lunch. What must have been a cup of tomato soup, a reddish pool full of shards of porcelain. An exploded sandwich, the top of one half of it dangling from the chair arm. Coffee splashed on the bedspread, the cup snuggling against the pillow, intact.

Dirt in Mouse's hair, on her cheek, her arm, her orange blouse. A Mouse no longer cool, but savage, lip lifted over clenched teeth, an alarming expression if anything like a face, another face, could any longer alarm.

Rob, up now, arm around her shoulders, supporting her, felt her start to shake. He lowered her into the chair. Madeline with a kind of remote interest watched him visibly attempting to pull himself together, trying to adjust his body to wariness, strength, composure.

"Bloody bitch," through the teeth, "she's *really* ruined everything—"

"First of all, shut up," he said. "One way or another, it's us against him now. And she only did what you would have done, only you'd have done it with a bullet maybe, not

flubbed it like she did. Of course she didn't know about your
friend Al, it might have worked otherwise."

"Worked for her, worked for *you*," Mouse said with the
rage of the trapper trapped. Madeline in her shock only
partially understood her.

"I said, shut up. Ma, *please* stop shaking . . ." He went and
got her two aspirins and filled her thermos cup with water.
She obediently took them while he held the cup to her lips.
Her hands were in no state to hold it without splashing.

Rain hit the windows facing northeast as though hurled
from a bucket. Rob went to the clear window and stood looking out, and down. Mouse moved to his side and looked down
too.

"He's too dangerous for her to be left to him," she said.
Flat, frank, practical statement. Merchandise again, Madeline
thought. I'm worth money, lots of it, now what are they going
to do?

"Kind of a rough drop, from here," Mouse mused. "About
what? Ten or twelve or more feet, and you'd have to land
with each foot sort of sideways because of the roof peak
you'd have to straddle it . . . and it's probably slippery with
the rain and all . . ."

She made a little choked laughing noise. "Looking ahead
we go to jail, he stashes away the money, if the police get to
talk to him he doesn't know what they're talking about. He's
wiped away all his fingerprints. You wrote the note and then
threw in a personal chat with your father. God, it couldn't be
more *beautiful*."

"So?" Rob asked in a shorthand way.

"So, you won't leave your dear ma alone with me after
what she did." Mouse put a tender and loving hand to her
own shoulder.

"*And*, you're his friend, from the good old days of the
Mouse and Al Memorial Couch. The only problem is, would
you decide to play it his way?"

"The only problem besides broken ankles, you mean, or

lipping and crashing to the ground. —No, don't worry. I
night if there was any point in it but he'd take it all, can you
ee an Al Madonna doing a Boy Scout fifty-fifty split? And
vhat do I do, go to the police and say I've been robbed of
alf my kidnap money?"

Rob was unwiring the window latch. "I can lean out and
elp drop you."

"No. You're still sick as a dog—you'd damn well better be—
nd she can't make it at her age. And I've been thinking . . .
ou knocked me out cold last night, I wondered why I'd slept
ike the dead . . ."

Madeline listened to this conversation of so-called young
overs; she should have been trying to fill in the bits she
ouldn't understand but her mind refused right now to make
he effort.

"The sleeping pills," Rob said.

"Yes. I'm his cook. Italians never heard about women's lib.
Or not this one." She took off her thong sandals. "Better bare-
oot."

Rob opened the window. "Bon voyage, Mouse," breathless
vith urgency.

She got nimbly onto the sill, backed out, and hung for a sec-
nd by her hands, looking in at them. "Horrible fate, to have
een shot in the ass," she said merrily, and Madeline saw that
he was happy again, radiantly alive again, on her diet of
anger.

From his vantage point, Rob reported, "Landed okay . . .
Cod, he must have been waiting on the porch—"

They both listened for the sound of a shot and heard only,
uring the long, long moment, the rain.

Clinging to the streaming roof shingles with her palms and
alves and buttocks, Mouse inched her way down the slope,
vatching Al watching her, gun steadily ready. He stood a few
eet out from the porch steps.

When she reached the edge of the roof, she turned over,

slid deliberately until her fingers caught the edge of the
painted water spout, and let herself hang. There was a faint
protesting creak from the spout, but it held. She dropped to
the porch roof, turned around, sat on its edge, and said to Al,
"If you'll come partway up the steps and give me a hand—"

He did; she leaped, and the shock of hitting the ground ran
from her feet to her head.

With grudging admiration, he said, "You were asking for it,
Mouse, in every way. You could have broken your neck."

"I don't run with losers," Mouse said. "And yes, I wouldn't
have taken any bets on me getting down. We're changing
partners, okay?"

"I thought we already had." He put his gun back in his
pocket.

Side by side, they went up the porch steps and into the hall.
Al gestured her toward the living room, cautious warder as
well as flattered male joined by a girl who left the loser
behind.

"I was just having some gin, I found it under the sink,
don't suppose you want any?"

"No, thanks." Mouse walked into the darkened room,
turned on a lamp, casually shed her clothes, said, "I'm all dirty
but it's nice clean earth dirt," and lay naked waiting for him
on the sofa.

"I don't know," hungrily. "That kid."

With entirely convincing contempt, Mouse answered, "He
couldn't even help me out the window, the shape he's in. And
besides, do you think he'd dare leave his mother all by herself
with *you* around? You that said she'd be all right as long as
you didn't see her."

"Okay, fly now, pay later," Al said, dimpling and grinning,
"I mean, you will. Exactly when, exactly where, tonight's little
pickup job . . . because who knows who's going to make it
through today? You can hand it all over to me, Mouse. After
wards."

He stripped and joined her on the sofa.

During the entertaining exercise, Mouse thought flickeringly, God, how do crooks make money and get away with things when they're so *dumb?* Get moving, Rob. I know and you know you're not sick at all, Robbie. I'm doing my part. You do yours.

It was the first time that they had been alone in each other's company since a safe quiet disastrous evening in Morton Street.

A curiously empty room with two people in it, not wanting their eyes to meet.

Rob stood a long time at the window, mind waiting, emptied, hands deep in his pockets. These cutoff flannel shorts, that Al was going to burn later—why? Oh, yes, something about fingerprints.

From behind him, a quiet deliberately uncaring voice asked, "Why the collapse on the bed, when he was taking over? Not that anyone would walk straight at a gun, but . . ."

"I'm supposed to be poisoned. Because of the rats."

"Rats?"

"Mouse's rats. She made them up, but they sent an exterminator because the real estate people want to take people through the house and you were here and . . . anyway, I was down with the rat poison. Down where you were." He turned and faced her, eyes naked. "It's crazy, isn't it?"

This seeming to be a point not open to debate, Madeline picked up her book from the arm of her chair and said, "As we may have to spend hours together and as we have nothing whatever to say—" and started reading.

He looked at the mess on the floor and began ineffectually trying to clean it up with the ancient bathrobe from the closet.

On his knees and over his shoulder he said tonelessly, "Ma, I was coming up to take you away, out, last night, send you home, when he came down at me. He had a knife he knows what to do with, and I thought I wouldn't be much good to you dead. Not that any of that matters."

"Oh, well . . . I suppose . . . thank you," she said, and was surprised by the flare of warmth under her ribs.

The vagueness of her voice was a warning to her. Time hadn't stopped, unreality hadn't really taken over. Things, events, disposals were stored, waiting, in the very near future, one hour, four—? Maybe he'd wait until dark.

She said carefully something that had to be said no matter how impossible. "But you were in charge of my release and delivery arrangements and now he's in charge of them. I saw his face when he saw me—as though we'd both made some sort of horrible mistake. Because of course I can identify him. Which is the one flaw in Mouse's adjective, beautiful."

This time, looking at her, his eyes and face had a cleansed, clearing expression.

"A horrible mistake," he said. "Yes, I see what you mean, Ma. Do you mind being left alone for a few minutes?"

While she was saying in thoughtless astonishment, "But I *am* alone—" he had jackknifed his way backward through the window.

He was a good forty pounds heavier than Mouse and when his sneakers straddled the roof peak he slipped to the left and almost fell. A grab at the roof peak saved him.

He had no plan and no weapon, except to make an immediate weapon of himself and deal with Al, forthrightly and finally. It shouldn't be too hard, when there was no fear or feeling, or anything at all in him, but his one purpose.

Mouse might need hours to do her sleeping-pill trick, if she could pull it off at all. At any moment in any one of those hours Al might decide, Well, hell, get it over with—

Make it to the ground safely, though, no point in tumbling helplessly— The near fall had shaken him and he drew a few deep breaths and thrust dripping hair out of his eyes.

Knowing Mouse, he thought she might take the quickest and most obvious way of showing Al she was his devoted friend. How long had it been since she went out the window?

Twenty minutes or so. Probably too late now to seize that particular advantage. If Al at any second came out to check on his remaining two prisoners, he could always be leaped or dived upon. Let's see, 168 pounds ought to make a good dropped bomb. For her own practical reasons, Mouse would probably rally round, and then it would be two of them against one.

Sitting, he went carefully and lithely down the roof. Bad moment when he had to turn his back and hang from the spout, and then there was a great tearing screeching sound and the spout broke off in his hands—a ten-foot length of it— and he dropped hard to the porch roof.

Jesus, the *noise*, the wake-the-dead noise—

Without conscious thought, he slid his hand along the length of the spout until he held it about a foot from the end. The other end, ripped metal, was jag-toothed.

A door opened below, the porch door. Al ran down the steps and turned, facing him, with his gun. He was barefoot and wore, with his denim jacket, yellow and white striped undershorts, and should have looked comical; and didn't.

"I would've thought you'd have wanted to stay with your mother," he said. "What are you, crazy or something?"

Rob walked to the edge of the roof and looked down at him. "This damn thing broke—" and put all the power of his body into the swing of the spout.

Almost simultaneously, the jagged end caught Al on the side of the head and his gun went off. Rob didn't know who was screaming, was it him, was it Al? He crashed bleeding from the porch roof to the ground, to the tune of the screaming.

Oh God, what now? Mouse thought, her back pressed hard for support against the front door. She looked through the porch screen at Rob, on his face, one arm at an odd angle, and Al—God, all that blood around his head and neck—lying on his side. Two silences in the windswept rain.

I can't call a doctor—and they're too heavy to be dragged in out of the rain—

Exposure.

Bleeding to death.

What if someone, passing in a car, on Bellamy Road, heard the shot, and the screaming, and turned in at the drive-way . . . ?

She was all alone now, alone with the two who might already be dead, and that woman upstairs.

As in a terrible dream resumed after a brief unhelpful waking, a car came up the driveway, a black Mercedes.

Mouse fingered the doorknob behind her and melted into the darkness of the hall. From the tiny gap in the living-room curtains, she saw the car doors open and two men fling themselves out. Not passing strangers, not with those frantic faces—

That one, the dark one, had to be Rob's father. Same forehead, same nose.

Her shoes were upstairs, too bad. She snatched up her yellow canvas beach bag and went through to the kitchen. There was a plaintive meow, and her cat twisted softly against her ankle.

"Bye-bye, kitty, I hate to leave you," and she chanced an extra few seconds to put down a brimming saucer of milk, and then went out the back door into the rain.

She knew from childhood that across Farricker Road there was a deep belt of birch woods, and beyond that a pond with a sagging boathouse at its far end. That would do to hide in for the moment. If it was still there.

They'd be busy, those two men, with those two—bodies, were they?—for a while, and with getting Mrs. Devore out, if by now she wasn't a screaming zombie beyond any real saving. She must have seen at least some of it, and heard the shot and the awful noises of pain, who from?

Maybe, she thought, running swiftly through the birches, they won't call the police immediately, with Rob dying or dead, his mother maybe intact, money intact, but then something had to be done about bloody Al . . .

Hurry, run faster. She had five dollars in her jeans pocket. There was, not too far away, that sort of nice nutty boy in his garage studio in New Hope. He didn't really like anybody much either. He'd give her a bed, shelter, while she went about erasing herself and starting all over.

Lissa would be a nice name. Lissa . . . well, play it safe, Smith.

Get lost, Mouse.

The jut of the porch roof hid Rob, and whatever had happened to Rob, from her, but she thought the echoes of the shot and the crescendo noises of physical anguish would go on forever, bouncing back from the walls at her. In a paralysis of terror, she was quite unable to scream herself or make any sound but a quailing moan.

Rob gone, lost forever, lost even more than he'd been when she gave him from her bitterness those scalding last words, ". . . but I *am* alone . . ." denying him the fact of his own existence.

No point in dashing herself, breaking herself, against the door. No point in an alpine expedition out the window, down to the roof where she had seen him just barely rescue his own strong young body from slipping, falling.

No point in anything, except that now she was alone here, really alone, with that girl. And that man, who proclaimed silently, intimately, that he and she were both punished, and in for something large and difficult, when their eyes met.

She had no recollection of flinging herself on her bed but came to an awareness of her body there, curved, arms clinging to herself, in a storm of weeping, when she heard the sounds of two car doors slamming.

The weapons told their tale.

Al, sharp pocked silent face, gun near his inert hand,

efficient professional knife half out of his jacket pocket. The spout end inches away from his neck, Rob sprawled half over the spout—

"He must have fallen off the porch roof," Titus said, and "Oh Christ, I hope it isn't the heart," turning him over and seeing the blood. "Some kind of mortal combat, some kind of duel, over—"

"*Hughhhh . . .*" Lost-sounding wail from high above.

Bending over Rob, Devore looked up and saw her in the window, or a mask of pain and distress that resembled her, and burst into the house. Mouse, when for her it was all over, hadn't troubled to lock the door.

He ran up the stairs and, sweet sound to her, shot the bolt. He was unable to speak and neither was she but the fierce warm arms about her gave her back in this desolate place roof, walls, floor, and hearth fire.

Titus, cursing the rain, went about his business of hearts and pulses. The dark one's—who the hell was *he?*—strong, but he suspected mild concussion. Just in case, he turned him over on his face and tied the wrists together with his handkerchief.

Rob, he wasn't so sure about. On the one hand this, on the other hand that. The bullet had gone through the ribs, to the left, and might or might not have grazed the heart. He was bleeding dangerously. In his experience, it would probably amount to—surgical skills or not—did he want to stay alive, or didn't he?

Devore came down the porch steps, holding Madeline, holding her up. She thought that by now all her tears had been used but more fell on Rob's face as she knelt over him.

His lashes moved a little. She said, "I didn't mean that, about being all alone, you were with me, and you'd tried to . . ."

"We passed a halfway decent-looking motel in Newton," Titus said. "Take her there for now, Hugh, get her warm. I'll stay here and see to things for the moment. Just in case this

young crook-looking chap has cut the telephone wires, stop at
the nearest phone booth and send along the police, with a
doctor and an ambulance."

He looked at their two faces and to spare himself from the
radiance and the cutting grief looked away, and down again
at Rob.

Something about *his* face—some kind of stirring, strength-
ening, hanging on.

Broken and bleeding, their kidnapping son. Golden and
brown and soaked with rain.

Wisely and delicately, as he gestured them toward the car,
Titus said, "Perhaps—and it's a big perhaps—he's not entirely
beyond repair."

23

Mr. Cove rapidly came to regard the Devore kidnapping as his own and special personal crime, in a dollars-and-cents business way.

At first it had its drawbacks, the cars of the curious jamming the driveway, trespassers roaming, staring. The Prudence police obligingly supplied a sergeant so that there wouldn't be breaking and entering and removal of souvenirs.

He was well aware that most of the sudden crowd of customers interested in buying the house were fakes, and merely wanted to look it over and tell their friends about it. But he kept his patience, and a week after the Thursday when the ambulance had sirened its way through the quiet town, heading for the Aston place, his perseverance was rewarded.

The Ballards were in their fifties. He was a successful songwriter and his wife had inherited a string of immensely profitable surgical supply houses. They exuded to Mr. Cove a strong sweet scent of money; and what in this case was a help, a bored searching for novelty, excitement.

He pricked up his ears when he heard the woman behind him, on the stairway, mutter to the man, "I mean, how fabulous for cocktail parties and weekend guests and things—"

They had read about the aborted kidnapping in the newspapers, and seen the house, and the faces, on television, but didn't have all the details at their fingertips. Mr. Cove did.

"Now—another flight but worth it—if you'll follow me, this is the room where she was kept after they took her out of the cellars."

Mrs. Ballard was thrilled by the olive and purple gloom. "*What* a guest room. Can you imagine people telling people they'd actually *slept* in it?"

"Good idea to leave things as they are for a while, not change anything," said her husband, "—*if* we decide to buy it, that is. At least the vital rooms. Sort of like a museum."

On the way into the house, they had both surreptitiously eyed the gravel near the porch steps; but there was no blood any longer to be seen.

"This black overall suit," Mr. Cove said, while showing one of the large second-floor bedrooms, "was Rob Devore's. I saw him wearing it. Playing poker with that girl in the living room. Poker. With his own mother more or less in chains."

"Handsome kid," Ballard said. "What'll he get, d'you suppose?"

"Well, now that he's off the critical list he'll be heading for some kind of prison term, probably, but," Mr. Cove added judicially, "there are extenuating circumstances. Mrs. Devore said he tried to stop the whole thing in the middle and let her go, but then this Madonna fellow moved in. Had a whole arsenal of weapons with him, knives, guns."

"I bet the courts won't be so nice and kind to him as they may be to the Devore kid. Armed and all—he shot the boy, didn't he?—and from his pictures he looks like a tough customer, dark-alley kind of guy." Ballard paused, repeated his last phrase, and said, "Already this house is good luck, I think I've got me a song. Might be another Mac the Knife," and he started to hum a little under his breath.

"The kitchen," Mr. Cove said, waving an arm and deciding to risk adding twenty thousand to the asking price. "The prisoner's meals were prepared at that stove. Bought new last year."

"Prepared by that girl . . . what? Mouse? Have they found her?"

"No." Mr. Cove gave his mind a little flight. "By now she may be in New Orleans, or Quebec—or Canberra, Australia. I guess there's something to be said about them all looking like everybody else. From their point of view. Notice this tile floor, laid just a year and a half ago. Expensive work, but these things pay off."

As they were about to descend to the cellars, there was a meowing at the back door. Mrs. Ballard opened it and the cat came in and went instantly to an empty saucer under the kitchen table.

"That cat," Mr. Cove invented, for color, "belonged to Madonna. His mascot, you might call it."

"How nice!" Mrs. Ballard said. "A sort of household god or goddess, we'll see . . . It must have been lonely here for the poor thing after all those people—uh—went away and left it. Consider yourself adopted, kitty."

A FEW CLUES ABOUT MORE GREAT TITLES YOU'LL SOON BE SEEING IN KEYHOLE CRIME

THE TWELVE DEATHS OF CHRISTMAS
Marian Babson

In the hectic days just before Christmas a series of random and bizzare killings transfixes London and presents the police with an insoluble problem.

Superintendent Knowles must pinpoint and catch one crazed but outwardly normal person at large in the vast metropolis, and it is not until the Christmas dinner gathering in a London house that he realises the last of the twelve deaths of Christmas is about to take place...

MOTIVE IN SHADOW
Lesley Egan

When Claire Manning dies, her will says that a distant third cousin is to inherit everything. Her son John, who has been running the prosperous Manning business for years is incredulous and hires a lawyer-detective to find out why she should have done such a thing. Step by step the investigation uncovers a remarkable tale of blackmail and impersonation reaching back into Claire's distant past.

 Keyhole Crime

FATAL SWITCH
Ian Stuart

Accidents will happen even in the best regulated companies and so when a scaffold tower collapses killing an employee at Bruces, everyone is satisfied that it is a tragic accident. But then a rumour spreads that Bruces is in financial trouble, Neil Bruce surprises an intruder and a lorry is hijacked. Someone is out to smash the firm – but who and why? Neil Bruce tries to find out before his company is ruined.

CHILL FACTOR
Aaron Marc Stein

Heading north to Vermont for a skiing holiday, Matt Erridge finds himself in the middle of a blizzard. When his car skids into a snowdrift he sets off on a little unscheduled cross-country skiing and comes across another stranded motorist – recently deceased. Rescued by a good Samaritan, Erridge finds he is a guest at an impromptu house-party – where it is obvious that death rides the storm.